JENNY ON THE STREET

AND OTHER TALES OF REVERENCE AND REVOLUTION BY A VERY YOUNG MAN

DAVID HALDANE

Black Rose Writing | Texas

ISBN: 978-1-68433-642-5
PUBLISHED BY BLACK ROSE WRITING
www.blackrosewriting.com

Printed in the United States of America
Suggested Retail Price (SRP) $14.95

Jenny on the Street is printed in Calluna

*As a planet-friendly publisher, Black Rose Writing does its best to
eliminate unnecessary waste to reduce paper usage and energy
costs, while never compromising the reading experience. As a
result, the final word count vs. page count may not meet common
expectations.

To my beloved daughter and editor, Adina Haldane Morgan, who, despite all evidence to the contrary, still believes in her old man. Without her wisdom and support, this book might never have seen print.

Disclaimer

I did not write these stories. In fact, they were composed by a much younger man who bears my name. I was not even aware of the material's existence until coming across it quite recently, buried deep in the back of an old file cabinet where the author had apparently stashed it years before. Though we had a nodding acquaintance in those days, I have no actual recollection of him ever penning these tales. While some are clearly fictional, others are, well...somewhat less so. In this respect, I believe, they mirror the modern age in which the line between reality and fantasy has become increasingly blurred. I therefore leave it to individual readers to locate that line for themselves.

I am publishing the stories now, in the hope that someone somewhere will find them entertaining and/or instructive. Though diverse in content and style, these thirteen fables share at least one common thread: a reflection of the epoch in which they were born. It was a magical time when events were surreal, feelings magnified, and change was in the air; an era, I might add, not unlike our own.

For ease of reading and comprehension, I have divided the stories into separate sections: Time and Space. The first contains yarns fairly easily placed within those parameters. The second, well, those not so bound. Without any further ado, let me get out of your way. I hope you enjoy these narratives and find them engaging. I'm confident the author, wherever he is, would like that too.

David Haldane
January 2021

JENNY ON THE STREET

CONTENTS

Part I
TIME

THE SUN'S TRUMPETER

Mornings you could see him from the boardwalk. See him, that is, if you happened to be up that early. A tiny, upright silhouette bathed by the endless orange of the sunrise over the sea. You couldn't tell what he was doing all alone on the beach at that hour. Probably nothing, you'd think. Perhaps he was just walking. It'd make a nice photo; wish I had my camera, you'd think. And then you'd hurry on your way because it had been a wicked all-nighter and you were eager to get home for some much-needed sleep. But long after you had gone, long after you lay dreaming comfortably in the mahogany bed next to your wife, the sad silhouette remained on the beach. Remained, outlined by the increasingly brilliant sunrise, like a stubborn matchstick in the corner of a fireplace refusing to be consumed by the fire it had kindled.

The first time Sean ever saw the gleaming trumpet, it had been sitting in the window of George's Loan & Music Co. on King Street. The boy's eyes had lit up, but he said nothing. Sean seldom *did say* anything. But it was enough to catch the attention of his grandfather, who stayed finely attuned to virtually *any* emotion that clawed its way to the surface of the young boy's face. "Do you like that trumpet?" the old man asked. "Would you like to take it home?"

As usual, nothing erupted from the boy's mouth. But the light in his eyes seemed to flare for an instant, just long enough to spark a decision on his grandfather's part. "Let's go in," he said. "Let's take a look." And that was the beginning of Sean's obsession with the ancient trumpet someone had hawked, and his grandfather had bought.

In the old man's view, it was an unlikely pairing. From the time, years before, that the boy's mother had dropped him off before disappearing into the ether that is the world, Sean had been an unusual child. To be honest, *odd* would be a more apt description. While other children played, this one seemed to brood. And when others spoke, Sean kept his silence. On more than one occasion, in fact, the youngster's strange aloofness had been noticed.

Once a school counselor came to see the grandfather with an alarming observation; perhaps, she said, the child was autistic. Maybe experts familiar with such conditions should do an evaluation. Even better, she said, why not put him in a special school equipped to deal with kids like him? But the grandfather had always rejected such suggestions, preferring to care for the boy himself. Finally, to avoid any further confrontations with authorities, he had withdrawn Sean from school altogether, declaring that he would educate him at home. And so it had gone, with the grandfather doing what he could while the youngster passed his days in bewildering silence.

Until the day he saw that trumpet. In the weeks that followed, a change came over the silent boy who by then had turned fourteen. Somehow, the grandfather thought, he seemed more alive, animated by some unseen purpose. And then the mysterious early morning sojourns began. At first, they seemed tentative; the grandfather would awaken to hear the boy leaving the house just before dawn. Fighting back the sense of panic swelling in his chest, the old man would lie still. The boy, he'd whisper into his own ear, must learn to fend for himself. And, indeed, Sean always returned; eventually the grandfather would hear the front door open and the boy's door close. And only then could he breathe easy knowing his grandson was safe.

But the daily journeys weighed on the old man's soul. What were they about, he wondered; where, exactly, did young Sean go? Was this just more inexplicable behavior or was something greater at stake? One morning he decided to find out. Arising early, the old man waited for the telltale sound of the front door opening. Then, quickly counting to fifty to give the boy a head start, he slipped into a pair of sweatpants and stepped out into the predawn dark. It took him a while to get oriented.

The world looked unfamiliar without the sun, and the old man had to pause long enough for the shadows to materialize into recognizable forms. Then he saw Sean, walking purposefully down the boardwalk with the horn tucked neatly under his arm. The grandfather followed, wondering where the walk would end. He didn't have to wait long; suddenly the boy halted, and much like a soldier on parade, did an abrupt *left face* and marched toward the ocean.

The grandfather did the same, staying just far enough behind to avoid detection. When the boy got to the water's edge he stopped, put his hand over his eyes, and peered into the distance as if looking for a sign. Then the hand stiffened into a salute and fell smartly to his side. Standing at attention with his feet planted firmly and well-apart in the sand, Sean solemnly lifted the trumpet to his lips and stood poised to blow.

A moment passed.

Then, as if emanating from some mysterious far-off place, a shrill note issued forth from the magic horn followed by several more in quick succession. The grandfather recognized the tune immediately;

he'd heard it many times in his youth. It was the sound to which he'd arisen each morning of the early military training that so many of his generation had endured; the boy was playing *Reveille*, the universal call to wakefulness heard now with a power and precision that weakened the old man's knees.

The grandfather watched as Sean belted out the tune. And suddenly, as if on cue, the first rays of the morning sun peaked out over the horizon, careening directly into the bell of the young boy's trumpet. For an instant, the horn shimmered with an ethereal radiance and the old man couldn't distinguish between it and the sun, could not be sure whether they were two objects or one. But it was only a spark. The moment passed. Sean played until the sun had fully emerged. Then fervently removed the horn from his lips and half-turned in the early light, revealing an expression of more complete happiness than the grandfather had ever seen.

As the old man shuffled back home, his eyes brimmed with tears. He had feared the worst, feared that the boy he loved had already left him for good. Instead, it seemed, he had found his purpose, one so grand that it couldn't be denied. Sean was the sun's trumpeter. The old man smiled to himself as the smooth, warming sand squished through the spaces between his toes.

THE LAST CLARINET LESSON

I used to wake up on Saturday mornings with a knot in my stomach. Thinking it was indigestion, I'd peel myself out of bed and make my way to the toilet, but it never helped. There was nothing to do on those mornings but shuffle into the kitchen and not eat my breakfast. Mom wouldn't say much, just make a show of getting her car keys out of the kitchen drawer and, before I could say "Mozart," I'd be on my way to my weekly clarinet lesson.

God forbid anyone should think I didn't enjoy being a clarinetist. I was first chair in my high school orchestra and that felt pretty darn good. In a few weeks, I was scheduled to solo with a Mozart Concerto, and everyone would congratulate me and comment on my talent. Whenever we performed, Mr. Sandberg, the music director, would ask me to play a long *Concert A* to which everyone else would tune their instruments.

AAAAAAAA, I would blow (*what clarity*). AAAAAAA (*what grace*). AAAAAAAAA (*oh hear me sweet violinists*). *AAAAAAA* (*oh listen up sexy flautists*). *AAAAAAA* (*oh pay attention Mr. Sandberg*).

No, the fact was that I liked *being* a clarinetist; it was just *practicing* the clarinet that didn't tickle my fancy.

Mr. Palin seldom met me at the door for my lesson. Usually it was his wife, an exceedingly plump woman very fond of run-on sentences. "Good morning dear, you're early. Walter will be with you in a minute, just wait in the studio." Then she'd waddle down the hall, her extraordinary rump seeming to wink at me with every step.

The studio was a small den that always smelled of cork grease. That's the putty used to lubricate the joints of a clarinet. I loved the smell of cork grease; it's one of those sweet, faraway whiffs that carry you away with it, not unlike the odor of airplane glue. The kind of smell that makes you forget things like knots in your stomach and confusion in your cords. Cork grease can do strange things to your head too; a fact explaining, I eventually surmised, why so many clarinetists sway as they play.

The studio was sparsely furnished, containing only four pieces. In the corner sat a small table on wheels supported by a too-heavy old-fashioned record player. And placed mathematically in the center of the room stood two folding chairs and a music stand. That was all; the rest was bare, save the walls. I would sit awkwardly on one of the chairs and, feeling the euphoric effects of the cork grease coming on, stare in fascination at the walls displaying the proud mementos of Mr. Palin's lengthy career.

There was a diploma framed in gold: Cincinnati Conservatory of Music, 1915. To its right hung a large photograph of the old New York Philharmonic Orchestra with a figure I recognized as Arturo Toscanini, the famed Italian conductor, at the podium. In the lower right-hand corner, scrawled in an almost illegible hand and faded ink: "To Walter Palin–one of the finest musicians it has been my pleasure to work with. With gratitude and respect, A. Toscanini. September 1930."

There was also a blue ribbon inscribed: "Walter Palin, for superb musicianship and performance, National American Music Festival, Buffalo, N.Y. 1921;" a yellow newspaper clipping showing a much-younger Mr. Palin shaking hands with an unidentified conductor headlined, "Walter Palin Congratulated on Superb Weber Performance"; and a small golden certificate dubbed, in old English lettering, "Certificate of Recognition and Gratitude" and sealed with the insignia of the NBC Orchestra, Hollywood, California, 1950.

Looking at Mr. Palin's wall always reminded me of his favorite story, often told in his unabashed Midwestern drawl. "On the day I was born, my father put a clarinet in my mouth, gathered all the neighbors around and declared, 'See how well it goes? He likes it already! My son will be a great clarinetist!'" Mr. Palin would slap his knee enthusiastically. "'My son will be a great clarinetist,' my father said."

At about that point in my meditations, the door would invariably open and in would waddle the old man himself. He was eighty-three and looked it. "Good morning David," he'd say with a grin that only an 83-year-old clarinetist who had played under Toscanini could muster. "Are you warmed up yet?"

And as I awkwardly fumbled for an excuse to explain why I wasn't, the old man would gingerly grasp his trousers just above the knees, pull them up over his ankles and huff to a sitting position on the folding chair next to mine, which was a considerable feat as he was almost, though not quite, as fat as his wife.

I knew damned well I hadn't yet warmed up. I also knew that if I stalled long enough, Mr. Palin would have his instrument out and warmed up before me and, once the old man got that thing into his mouth, it'd be a long while before he took it out again. For me, that was a vacation. I'd sit there listening contentedly, happy to postpone the moment of truth when he would finally hear my lessons and pass judgment on how well I'd practiced.

It wasn't hard listening to him play. That man could blow one hell of a horn. He looked ridiculous sitting there, like a fat toad sitting on a mushroom drawing the smoke of some exotic foreign tobacco from the business end of a water pipe. He looked like a character from *Alice in Wonderland*. But then he'd start playing, and the sound coming out of that water pipe was mellow and pure. The truth was that I could spend hours listening to him blow, buoyed by those sweet tones floating in the air amidst the smell of that wonderful cork grease.

He'd sit there playing for a while, making a river out of what for me had been a glass of water, and then he'd stop and turn to me with a gleam in his eye. He'd look at me triumphantly, fairly choking on his own emotion, and breathlessly gasp, "Did you hear that, boy? That's how you play the clarinet! That's how it should sound. Someday you'll play like that, son. I will make you an artist!" He'd lift his hands and, holding them dramatically aloft, make a gesture of cradling my face. Then he'd focus his eyes on what seemed like a point about three miles beyond the back of my head. "I will make you a brilliant artist, my boy. I promise."

And so it went.

One Saturday in the spring of my senior year, something unsettling occurred; I found both Mr. *and*

Mrs. Palin waiting for me in the living room where they had set up a makeshift studio. As they ushered me in, I couldn't help but notice the pungent aroma of alcohol overpowering everything, including that soothing cork grease smell. It thrust itself into my nostrils, devilishly tickling the nerve endings there, determined to make its presence known and unrelenting in its desire to betray the old man.

Mr. and Mrs. Palin sat on the couch, blurry-eyed and red-nosed, their faces looking like marshmallows roasted and forgotten. It was as if the party was over and the guests had gone home, leaving these two roasted marshmallows lying squashed and abandoned among the debris. A cold depression lay about the house like a heavy medallion on the neck of an Olympic swimmer who'd just lost the race.

I had never seen them like this before and felt disconcerted. I wished I were somewhere else, somewhere far away. I distrusted melancholy old men–especially clarinetists–who changed their mood the way other people changed their underwear. I disliked the smell of ether emanating from the old man's mouth like a foreboding cloud.

I might have escaped, had I not already tarried too long. The old man eyed me sadly and his words escaped like the last members of a crew evacuating a sinking ship. "H... hello there *shun*. Shit down and *worm* up." In their eagerness to escape, the words tumbled over each other in numb confusion on the way out. "D..don't mind *ush*," he said. "J.. just s.. sit down and *worm* up."

His breath smelled like the formaldehyde jar in which I'd gassed butterflies as a child.

As I fumbled nervously with my clarinet, Mr. Palin riffled through my folio, finally withdrawing a sheet of music. It was the Mozart Concerto that had been there for months, the piece I should have been working on for the upcoming concert. As with everything else in my folio, though, I had worked on it only sporadically and with significant pain. Mr. Palin turned the pages to the third movement, a solemn processional done entirely in 4-4 time, all in the lower register. It was the saddest piece of music in my folio.

"Play this for *ush*, *shun*," he said, smiling at me faithfully like an old dog about to be fed. Then he sat down on the couch directly opposite the folding chair on which I sat, put his fat arm around his wife's fat shoulder, and together they waited for me to begin.

There would be no escape. I swallowed the lump that had lodged itself in my throat, put the clarinet to my lips, took a deep breath and blew. I had barely completed three bars when Mr. Palin stopped me. "Please, my boy. This is a slow and beautiful tune. Play it with grace. Play it with *feeling*. Begin again..." His manner was direct. I had never seen him like this. I began again.

"To play a single note and, with it, lend some clarity to the chaos in the listener's soul," he had always told me. "That is the mark of a skilled musician. Tone, clarity, purity, simplicity–the four requisites."

But he stopped me again. And when I considered his face this time, I saw tears in his eyes. "Please, my son. Do you love your mother? Play this for your mother."

And I tried, but again he interrupted. "For the love of God then, dammit, for the love of art!" His old tear-brimmed eyes pleaded desperately. "A great musician does not merely *play* music, he *lives* it. He *is* his music. Don't just play music, be a *musician*." This too I had heard before but, apparently, hadn't learned. A cold fog of dread began forming in my chest, hanging there like the first signs of cancer. And suddenly I knew the truth; that giving him what he wanted required more than I could spare.

When he stopped me the fourth and final time, I knew just how it was. "For the love of life," he pleaded. He tried to choke back a sob but failed. It escaped and, with it, others. It was as if someone had pulled a plug from the old man's soul. "You... You can go now." He buried his face in his hands and gave up trying to choke back the drunken sobs.

I could hear the wind outside, knocking on the door. I answered the knock, and the wind brushed past me, silhouetting my exit. Stealthily, I stepped onto the sidewalk and wiped the old man's tears from my shirt sleeve.

I never went back to Mr. Palin's. And in the years that followed, the main thing I remembered was the sweet, mind-bending smell of that intoxicating cork grease.

THE SERGEANT

"Have another hit," said the sergeant, and he handed the pipe across the table to the uniformed private who, glancing furtively about like a boy caught masturbating, reluctantly put it to his lips and took a draw. "Private Tooley here ain't done much smoking," chuckled the sergeant, looking at me. Then he glanced back at Tooley and his smile disappeared. "Ain't you Tooley?"

But Tooley's boyish face stayed puckered, his eyes red and watery.

"Ain't you Tooley?" the sergeant demanded.

The boy exhaled and a huge stream of smoke billowed out of his mouth, hovered like an enormous spider over the table, then dissipated. "No, sir." He passed the pipe to me.

"The trouble with these young'uns we get today," said the sergeant, looking at me, "is there's no backbone in 'em. No balls. You know what I mean?" I nodded. "Hey buddy, how you like the shit? I'll tell you a secret," he said, nudging me hard in the ribs. "This here's the best shit in Berlin."

I passed him the pipe. "Mind telling me where you got it?" I was curious how the hell a redneck military dude had gotten hold of such excellent hashish.

Like a burglar alarm, he pounded the table gleefully, and I noticed the gaping blue and purple tattoo on his thick forearm. The sergeant was a powerful man, stocky, and looking at him I felt like I was facing a huge coiled spring that could be unleashed any second by the slightest unguarded movement. At times, the tension boiled up into his face in grotesque contortions, making his entire head a tremendous pressure dome ready to burst and immerse everyone in some kind of hot, sticky ooze.

"You hear that?" he said, jerking his thumb in my direction and looking over his left shoulder as if someone were sitting there. "The fella wants to know where I got it. Ha! You're gonna have to find your own connection, buddy."

"I didn't mean to pry."

"Forget it. Want a beer?"

"My throat's dry."

"Buy us two beers, Tooley, you can pay for 'em yourself. "

Relieved, Tooley pushed back his chair and bounded off towards the bar.

The sergeant took another long drag from the pipe and blew out the smoke. "I swear to Jesus, the kids we get in the service today are nothin' but a bunch 'a queers. How long you been in Berlin, buddy?" His eyes were swimming as he spoke.

"Couple 'a months."

"Thought so. Want some friendly advice? Don't talk so much."

"What?"

"You don't go sittin' at a pub in Berlin and askin' a man where he gets his dope. 'Specially a sergeant of the United States Army, understand? Not even in a fag joint like this."

"Why not? I'm sure none of these..."

"For Crissakes, what the hell you mean 'why not?' Look around you, buddy." He indicated the neighboring tables with an impatient sweep of his arm as if they were dust and his arm was a broom. "Take a look around and tell me what you see."

I did as he said. "Nothing. What are you getting at?"

He threw up his arms in exaggerated disgust. "Christ, you're being stupid. *Germans.* They're Germans, idiot, open your eyes." He was hissing at me like a broken gas line, and for the first time I felt real fear. "You spend any time here and you quickly learn that a kraut's a kraut and a human being's a human being. There's *us* and there's *them*, understand?"

At that moment, Private Tooley reappeared, carrying a tray with three beers. The sergeant clutched my arm and, softening, whispered almost affectionately into my ear. "Sorry I called you stupid, buddy. Listen, you ever want any dope you come to me, ok? I'll get it for you, all you need to do is ask."

Tooley set the tray down on the table and then sat down himself. The sergeant hardened as if a ghost had tapped him on the shoulder. He glared at the beers on the table, then at Tooley. "You don't hear too good, do you private?" Tooley stared uncomprehending. "How many beers did I order, Tooley?"

"Sir?"

"I said two beers, not three."

"Well, I thought I'd..."

"When I tell you to do something, don't think, Tooley, just do it. You ain't gettin' none." The corners of his mouth twisted into a malicious grin and his black eyes, swimming and streaked with red, jiggled in their sockets indicating wide circumferences as they struggled to remain pinned to the private's incredulous face. "You ain't gettin' no beer 'til you've finished your dope, my boy." He handed the pipe across the table, laughing. "Smoke up, Tooley. Your beer will stay on the floor 'til you've earned it. Unless

I get thirsty, that is. Better hurry. What're ya waiting for, boy?"

Private Tooley's eyes shone with genuine terror. "I can't smoke no more, Sarge. I got enough."

The sergeant hit the table hard with his fist. "Goddamn it, boy, better not be disobeying cuz if you are it'll go hard with you, I guarantee. Smoke!"

Tooley pursed his lips and stared into the bore of the pipe. When he looked up, there was a glint of hope in his eyes. "It's gone out, Sarge. There ain't no fire."

Something inside the sergeant snapped. "Get that goddamned pipe lit! I don't care if you have to rub two sticks together, dammit, get it done!" Grumbling, his forehead throbbing, he fumbled through his pockets. "No matches, Christ Almighty. No matches, shit!" He turned to me. "You got any matches, buddy?"

Tooley stared at me beseechingly. The sergeant repeated his request. "Got any matches?" I reached into my pocket fingering the matchbox there, and realized that I had come to a crossroads. In one direction lay the bright and well-paved road of fear; in the other, the darkened dirt path of courage. *Got any matches... any matches... matches?* A few seconds passed and my knees began to tremble. I hesitated, then took the well-lit road.

"Sure," I said, tossing the box of matches onto the table. The sergeant shoved them toward Tooley. With shaking fingers, the private lit the pipe and took a modest drag off it. The first time he choked and coughed up all the smoke, so the sergeant made him take another drag, then another, and another, and each time he made him hold in the smoke until he couldn't hold it any longer without suffocating. When it was all over, the boy's eyes looked like dried apricot seeds.

"How you feel now, boy?" asked the sergeant. Tooley didn't answer, just lay with his head on the table, moaning softly.

"You thought you could cross me, but you forgot one thing, didn't you boy? You forgot that I'm the sergeant. Ain't I?" Still no answer. The sergeant pulled the pipe from the boy's limp hand on the table and relit it. Then, turning my way, he casually flung his tattooed arm over my shoulders and pinned me with his eyes. "Ain't I?" he said, and I thought his beer breath would burn.

A few days later, I heard the news. A friend who enjoyed hanging out with soldiers passed it along; someone in the barracks had taken a bullet in the eye. "They think it was suicide," my friend said. "No one seems to know who the guy was; they think he was a private."

And that's when I realized that the trembling would never stop.

JENNY ON THE STREET

The girl had the greenest eyes I'd ever seen.

I met her in a youth hostel of Munich, one of those dreary places where foreigners gathered in summer to be awakened at seven a.m. by German marching music. The hostel was full, so I slept with a bunch of other hippies in a park across the street. But in the middle of the night it rained and we fled to the shelter of a walled construction site nearby. So in the morning we woke, not to the sound of bugle and drum, but to the steady hum of bulldozers slamming into the side of our wall, bricks dropping all around us like bombs.

Efficient people, the Germans.

She was from Vancouver B.C., and when the carnage ended and I sat on the hostel steps awaiting the crazy ride that would take me to Zagreb, she was sitting next to me rolling up her sleeping bag. The first thing I noticed was the peacock feather careening out of her hat.

"Hey, that's a feather," I said.

"Well, it ain't a banana."

But I think it was the eyes that called to me the loudest; little green gems surrounded by curly blonde locks. She was eccentric looking, wearing an Afghan coat with bellbottoms and that crazy feather, and right away I wanted some more.

"What you reading?" I asked, noticing the book in her lap.

She held it up for me to see and, had I needed any more convincing that the moment was providential, the book's title would have immediately provided it: *The Teachings of Don Juan; A Yaqui Way of Knowledge.*

In fact, I had read Carlos Castaneda's tome several times. It's the story of a young man's journey toward enlightenment and the Yaqui Indian sorcerer who helps him find his way. The book tells many tales; of hearing God's voice while eating peyote roots and flying like a blackbird after smoking Jimson weed.

It also contains a quote I had never forgotten: *Does this path have a heart? If it does, the path is good; if it doesn't, it is of no use.*

And so I knew I would see her again.

"You any good at untying knots?" she wanted to know, interrupting my reverie. She pushed the words out one by one with great care, as if each were a priceless piece of glass. I weighed them, examined them in the light for secret angles, and thought what a fine bracelet they'd make.

"Let's see what you got," I replied.

She shoved her half-rolled sleeping bag into the chasm between us and it hung there for a second, balanced precariously on the silence. When I touched it, she smiled, and I realized again that it was right. Just a typical scene in crazy Europe of a youth-hostel steps like it happened always. You didn't have time for preliminaries; either it was right, or it wasn't, and either way you accepted it and then moved on, you just moved on.

I remember a later time when I was sitting at a café in Athens and met a girl with whom to traverse the islands. She was twenty and good-looking and just out of college. On the two-day boat ride over the blue Aegean Sea, we shared a sleeping bag for warmth. We spread it out on the deck, laughing every time the spray hit us, thinking of Homer, thinking of Ulysses, and by the time we got to Tinos we were acting like young marrieds, renting a Greek lady's living room while she slept on the bathroom floor with the door shut between us.

And two days later, I woke up alone.

But it didn't surprise me because that's the way it was in Europe of a hippy summer when you had no place to arrive at or return to; life was fast and, though it felt sad, you held it in and went with the flow. And when the roaring got too loud in your head, there was nothing to do but shove in the earbuds and tighten up the suitcase lid.

So, Jenny and I were going in opposite directions, and that was that. She gave me an address in London, extracting a promise that I would look her up when I got there, and I assured her I would. And then we parted, she with her peacock feather that wasn't a banana; me with my sentimentality and madness rolled into one.

A lot happened to me then. I got a three-day ride through Yugoslavia with a crazy Afghani in a Volkswagen who kept driving up exit ramps. When we got tired, we'd sleep by the road and every morning he'd wake me at 6 a.m. with a bell, standing over me in his big white pants that looked like baggy pajamas.

"Rise up, my friend. We make go, no?"

But I won't tell you about that time because this is Jenny's story. I won't tell you about the women, and all the Greek liquor and the sand and the ocean and all the strange songs, and neither will I explain how the texture of my soul broke all physical laws by growing heavier the more widely it spread. No, this is Jenny's story, only hers. Three months after our meeting in Munich, I was in London.

And I called her.

And she said come over.

And I did.

Jenny lived in a part of town unfamiliar to me, which could have described pretty much *any* part of London. It took a lengthy subway ride to get there, almost to the end of the line. Then a walk along quiet streets lined with trees and quaint suburban houses. At last I found the number, unlatched the tiny wooden gate in the yard, shuffled up a pathway through the garden and knocked on the door. Almost immediately, the curtain behind the picture window in front flew open and there she stood minus the feather with an enormous grin on her face. She rapped on the glass and disappeared; then, a moment later, opened the door.

"Dave!" she said. "You made it!"

"As you can see."

She stepped aside and ushered me in. In the hallway, she gave me a hug and her grin was the biggest I'd ever seen. She took my coat and led me into a gigantic room, bereft of furniture.

"It's about time," she said. "Sit down. Tell me everything; where've you been?"

I glanced about the room, looking for a place to lay my backpack. Only two pieces of furniture were visible; a bed in the far corner and a couch closer by. "You don't know how miserable it's been here," she said, apparently noticing my confusion. "God, what a place; I thought I'd die."

Stacks of old cardboard boxes careened dangerously away from the walls. Yet, somehow, I knew they weren't hers. Across the room, nearly at the mouth of the vast fireplace, lay an enormous pile of clothing; pink bras, blue panties, dresses with frills.

"I've been in Greece," I said. "The Greek Islands."

I picked a spot next to the door and shed my backpack, then sat down next to Jenny.

"Greece, wow! Tell me all about it," she repeated. "I want to know *everything*."

She pulled out a pack of cigarettes and began smoking one shakily, exquisitely nervous like some delicate little animal. Her hands were thin as leaves. Tiny lines crept through them like miniature rivers.

"How long you been living here?" I asked.

She ignored the question. She didn't look as good as she had; she was thinner, and her clothes were too big. She was wearing a gypsy skirt that looked like it wasn't hers; baggy in the butt and so loose around the waist that she had to keep pulling it up to retie the rope she was using as a belt.

And the bones of her shoulders showed, edging their way through a 1920s shawl that was red, lacy, and inappropriate like a costume she'd picked out for a party to which only *she'd* been invited.

Her face, well, her face was still beautiful, but only under a yellowish pallor. And her sharp green eyes were less sharp and less green. She looked like she'd just gotten up. The edges of her eyes were crusty, and her teeth needed brushing.

"So how are you, tell me everything!" she said one more time with a familiarity that seemed slightly forced.

"Got any coffee?" I asked.

She stood up and slid out into the hall. "I share the kitchen with two other tenants," she said. "It's kind of like a rooming house."

As she turned to walk down the hall, I noticed the back of her neck. It was a thin neck, and a pale one; a child's moon neck that peeked meekly out from between two ample brushes of hair that looked heavier than the neck could support. As she walked away from me a breeze rattled the front door, got in somehow and brushed past her. The blonde fuzz on the back of that frail neck quivered slightly, and the red shawl drooped around her shoulders like a shroud.

So I was home again for a few days or a few weeks, and Jenny's neck and Jenny's face were to become familiar, as was the smoke of her cigarettes and the death in her eyes when she awoke in the morning. That first night when I asked her where I would sleep, she smiled and pointed to the couch catty-corner to the bed that was hers.

"Way over there?" I teased.

"Hey, you just got here man," she said, but underneath the feigned casualness I saw her cheeks flush. So I took the couch without another word and after the first night never thought much about it. And in the mornings when she dressed, she'd always ask me to look away as she stood before her vast pile of clothes like an animal trainer, hesitate a moment, then pick out a pair of somethings to slip into. "Hey, what you want for breakfast, man?" she'd say. "There ain't much, let me tell you..."

And at night before bed she'd stand there again, warming her hands as if the pile of old clothes were a fire and she was freezing. Then, forgetting about my gaze for a moment, or perhaps pretending to forget, she'd take off what she had on, fling it onto the pile like firewood and stand there naked, stretching out her arms, undulating towards it, swaying back and forth as if dancing to a strain of music that only she could hear. From where I sat, her tiny body looked exactly like a starving young boy's; flat and white and thin, bones showing, dainty blond hairs whispering over the skin of her buttocks. When she realized I was watching, she'd turn crimson and stumble into her coffee-stained nightgown, murmuring goodnight.

"How about eggs? You got any eggs?" I inquired.

She scrounged noisily through the refrigerator, knocking things over. As time went on, I realized that the pile of clothes in the living room was the only thing in the entire place that was really hers. And when I think of her today, I think of that pile, just a pile of old clothes in a huge empty room.

"Christ, I'm gonna have to go shopping," Jenny said. "I got some bread and butter; how about toast and coffee?"

I nodded my assent. And so we broke bread.

It was fall, and everyone was going home. In London, airport horror stories abounded; so-and-so had gotten there only to be told that the flight he'd booked through a travel office in town didn't exist and the office had disappeared. Entire families would be seated on their planes ready to go only to get yanked off at the last minute because the charter group through which they had booked was illegal.

But me, I was going to Iceland and for two reasons; first that I'd never been there and second that I'd never been there. Those were the days when life was about movement; sit still too long and you were bound to get old. The corollary was that if you could just keep moving, it would all last forever, that only when the scenery stopped changing would death darken your door.

There was also a practical reason I'd chosen Iceland; the airfare was cheap, and the flights were nonstop. I had a one-month visa for England, no work permit, less than half the price of the ticket, and food was expensive.

But there was a potential way out. I'd come across a sympathetic charter company that had given me a stack of leaflets. If I initialed each one and handed them out to tourists downtown, they would knock ten bucks off my fare for every leaflet resulting in a sale.

WARNING! the leaflets read. *As you read this, a hundred people just like you are getting screwed by unscrupulous charter flight operations; utterly ruthless people who use every trick in the book to lure you into their offices and squeeze money out of your wallet. Come into ours and we won't squeeze.*

Every morning after breakfast with Jenny, I'd grab the tube downtown and stand somewhere near the American Express building handing out leaflets. There were dozens of us doing it, though we knew it was illegal. Every few hours the cops would come by and, at least once a day, arrest someone who'd have to spend the night in jail. So I'd always wear my enormous Swedish Army coat with the huge pockets, and every time an American kid with a backpack walked by, I'd say out of the corner of my mouth, "New York, Boston, Montreal, Vancouver?" and if he hesitated or looked interested, I'd slip him a handbill bearing my initials. Then I'd turn the other way and walk fast.

The toast popped out of the toaster and, with her fingers trembling a little, she buttered it, put it on a plate and served it up along with a cup of coffee. Then, she sat down opposite me, nursing her cup, smiling, waiting for a reaction as if the piece of toast were an elaborate meal.

"Thank you," I said.

"That enough?"

"I never eat a big breakfast."

"Oh." She folded her hands around her coffee cup and stared into it, blowing softly onto the surface of the liquid.

"Watcha gonna do today?" she asked.

"The usual, I guess."

"Hand those things out?"

"Yup, but the progress is slow. I think lots of people just take them and throw 'em away."

"Oh." She continued blowing onto the black surface of her coffee, as if her breath were a breeze and the coffee a lake. "Why don't you stay in London a while?" she offered at last.

I responded only with silence.

"I'm going for a walk today," she said, "you could come. I could show you the city. There's a concert tonight; *Black Sabbath,* ever heard of them?"

"No," I lied, and immediately regretted it. Already I could feel that tug, the familiar tension between staying and leaving; the pull of my heart saying slow while my soul said to go.

"You could stay with me," she said, at last taking a sip of her coffee. The phone rang. Four times. Then stopped. "That's not for me," Jenny said.

"Look," I said, "I gotta get going. Best time for leafleting is in the morning."

"All right," she said.

I pushed my chair back, got up and sauntered into the hallway where my Swedish Army coat hung from a hook near the phone. I wrangled it off the hook, struggled with it, finally got it around my torso and checked the leaflets in the pocket. The coat was a gigantic thing with white fur inside that made me look like a Cossack. Jenny was still sitting at the kitchen table, staring impassively into space over her steaming cup of coffee.

"See you later," I said.

Outside it was beautiful with the morning sun glistening in from all angles in a myriad of colors. I walked down the path to the gate and was about to open it when I heard the faint call of my name from behind, turned around and saw Jenny standing in the doorway, framed by it, looking too frail to be there. "I'd go home," she said, "but it isn't home anymore, you understand?"

"I think so."

She kept looking at me a moment longer, her eyes thin like her neck, and then she smiled. "Never heard of *Black Sabbath*, huh?"

I insisted I hadn't.

So gradually time went by. I passed out my leaflets and, occasionally, I'd even sell one. Jenny never seemed to do anything for money, but always seemed to have a little, usually just enough to feed me. And gradually, penny by angry penny, Iceland grew near. And *Black Sabbath* was fine and so was Jenny, and eventually even the pile of clothing on the living room floor began looking like home. And at night there were concerts, lots of them, and Jenny always paid. She knew all kinds of people; sometimes we'd get in free because she knew a musician or a manager, someone she'd probably dated. And people started thinking of me as Jenny's old man.

One night a guy in a doughnut shop gave me a warning. "Listen brother," he said, "you got to watch out for this lady, dig?" It was Saturday night and we were looking for peyote, just like *Don Juan*. The guy was one of life's casualties, an old friend of hers, a man in his forties wearing a deeply creased face and long gray hair. "That girl likes to nibble," he insisted. "You gotta watch what she takes into her head, my friend. She'll nibble herself to death if you let her. And, for God's sake, keep her away from needles."

But he was just a drunk in a doughnut shop, and Jenny whisked me away after only one doughnut. Then I got my break. Three weeks to the day after arriving in London, four leaflets came into the office bearing my initials and I was over the top. Feeling ecstatic, I ran all the way home to tell Jenny the news; I'd be leaving on the first plane next day, airborne again and Iceland bound!

Jenny cried when I told her. She was sitting on that forlorn couch in the living room wearing the red shawl and the tears streaked her mascara until her face looked dark and needed washing. "Dammit, why do you have to go?" she wanted to know. She rubbed her eyes with the corner of the shawl and the words tumbled out like dirty water, soaking the red shawl with her grief. "What's there for you, man, I just don't understand...?"

"Neither do I," I admitted, "it's just that I got to go."

"But I need you here," she said. "Isn't that obvious?"

I was sitting next to her on the couch with her grip on my arm as tight as a vice. "What can I say, Jenny?"

"You're a sonofabitch."

"You knew I was going. I never told you I'd stay."

"Oh crap," she said. "Just shut up, you sonofabitch."

But after a while she stopped crying and went into the bathroom to wash her face. And when she came out, she seemed very calm. "All right," she said, "you win. I'm not gonna think about it anymore. We're going out tonight and we're gonna have a wonderful time."

"Anything you want, babe, and I'll even pay."

"That's a laugh," she said.

And it was.

We got duded up like we never had before and hit town. There was a pub nearby with an excellent band. Because she looked so young, she always had trouble getting in alone, but with me in tow nobody said a thing. The place was lit up and laid out like a circus sideshow. The customers sat on rows of wooden benches built up like a stadium grandstand. The floor was covered with a layer of sawdust, cut by the smell of booze. The musicians were superb, but it took them a while to get into it; by the end of the first set, they were beginning to warm.

Jenny seemed happy, seemed to have forgotten that this was our last night together, seemed to be swaying to the music, and I felt relieved. But the rafters were vibrating with a premonition of what was to come; had I looked up, perhaps I'd have noticed.

About halfway through the second set, she turned to me and very evenly said that she couldn't see.

"What?"

"I can't see, David, I mean it. Get me out of here."

I looked at her, thinking it was a joke, meaning to laugh, but the laugh never came.

"Are you on something?"

"Yes, dammit, get me out of here!"

Gingerly, I led her outside and when we got to the sidewalk, we stumbled down it and she seemed calm enough but kept saying that she couldn't see and when I looked into her eyes, I gasped because they were staring straight ahead into space, a horrified expression frozen onto them like ice. And when I waved my hand in front of her face, there was no response, not the slightest, nothing at all.

"All right," I said, "where do you want to go?"

"Home," she said, "just take me home."

So we walked toward the bus stop and the entire time my mind kept racing, trying to remember which bus to take from here, not knowing London at all, not remembering a thing. We stopped for directions. The guy pointed straight ahead. And Jenny slid through my arms in convulsions on the pavement.

At first, I thought she was dead.

She had fallen onto her back and the most horrible things were the eyes, the same ones I'd so admired on a morning that seemed long ago. Now they rolled upwards until only the whites were showing and her body arched off the pavement and her tongue wagged out of her head and saliva dribbled down her chin as if from a leaky faucet.

"Hold her tongue," somebody yelled.

I knelt beside her and felt for breathing. She was rigid, but her eyes still wriggled in their sockets. A crowd had gathered. I had no idea what to do. All I could see were belt buckles and shoes.

What do I do, what do I do? But nobody stepped forward. Everywhere, only silence rained down on my restless soul.

Suddenly a cab driver appeared. "Take us to the nearest hospital," I begged. It was the only thing I could think of. Together we must have gotten her into the back seat. The next thing I knew we were walking up a ramp through a swinging door that said *Emergency*. Jenny was on her feet now, thank God. She seemed to have at least one toe back in this world. But she still couldn't see, and kept screaming it out, flailing her arms wildly in front of her, feeling for the light. I had to hold her, or I don't know what she'd have done.

They got us into a little room and, after a while, an aide with a notepad came around and asked us our names. "Is the young lady on drugs?" he asked.

"I think so," I offered.

"What is she on?" he wanted to know.

"I have no idea," I said. "I'm really not sure."

"Hmm," he murmured, scribbling in the notebook. Then he smiled at me, a knowing smile, as if he and I were in this together and rather inconvenienced by such a bothersome situation. "Well, you try to keep her calm, all right?" he said, and that was the last we ever saw of him.

So I paced around, and held Jenny's hand, whispering into her ear. An hour later she was still blind as ever, beginning to sob now in low mournful tones, asking me over and over, "what am I gonna do, what am I gonna do?" And all I could say was "relax, babe, tomorrow you'll be fine," not quite believing it myself but wanting to make *her* believe it, and wondering whether anyone in the world would come to help this little girl, glaring at four hospital walls, staring into her horrific eyes.

And then, gradually, it came to me as a glimmer of recognition–all the days and all the nights and all the wars and towns and people and ways and all the years of madness–gradually it came to me that I would have to change my life, have to slow down, have to stay in one place long enough to breathe. It welled up in me like a mushroom cloud, all the poison blurting forth, all the sickness, and I knelt next to this little girl and said "Jenny, for Crissakes, it's enough already, let me take you home, let's just go home."

Her eyelids flickered and I thought maybe she would smile, maybe she'd say yes, but she didn't; her sightless eyes just kept flickering and her little chest heaved and a drop of spittle appeared at the corner of her mouth and the cells danced mirthlessly in her skin.

Random words filled my brain like bees from a hive. I stared at them, uncomprehending, until slowly they began forming sentences.

To seek freedom is the only driving force I know, Don Juan had said. *Freedom to fly off into the infinity out there. Freedom to dissolve; to lift off; to be like the flame of a candle. In a world where death is the hunter, there is no time for doubts.*

And so I flew to Iceland.

ISRAEL WOULD TAKE YOU IN, WOULDN'T IT?

The last time I saw Uncle Joe and Aunt Claire was the day my world collapsed. Wait, perhaps that's too strong; let's just say that my view of that world sustained a near-fatal blow.

It happened decades ago at their son's engagement party. Frankly, it was a parody of every Jewish party I'd ever attended, complete with strudel, kugel and kreplach. At least that's how it started. It ended differently, however, and fifteen minutes before the onslaught of the catastrophe that was to bisect our family forever, I lapsed into a reflective trance that only a well-aimed arrow could have pierced. Eventually one did, but that was still fifteen minutes in the future.

It had been years since I'd been to a synagogue. Because whenever you can, you forget the wailings of the centuries and, besides, I was only half Jewish.

Then one Friday night, a friend invited me to services and I found myself in a sea of Jewish faces. There were Yarmulkes and beards and strange black suits I'd seen previously only in the stories of Isaac Bashevis Singer and on the subways of New York. How foreign it all seemed, and yet how strangely familiar; a young man with a white face looked like a ghostly apparition about to turn on me and point a finger.

The praying began. We rose. The black-bearded rabbi stood at a podium, his back to us, praying in a torrent of Hebrew with his words flowing together in what, to me, formed a meaningless monotone. As he prayed, he bowed mechanically at the waist, like a wind-up toy. Next to me another man bowed mechanically to the Hebrew monotone, this one fatter, more robust, and more foreign looking. He bowed faster than the rabbi, as if racing toward the prayer's end, eager to finish with it and get some grub.

A flood of faces swept over me. One of them was the face of an old girlfriend, herself a Jew. Standing in the synagogue, I could see it now in the faces of these men, but it was a softer face, a delicate, beautiful face, a face that had whispered sweetly into my ear. On Friday Vermont evenings, we'd shared many suppers by candlelight to celebrate the Sabbath; her idea as I had never celebrated a Sabbath before. For me it was a novel experience; for her a gentler Sabbath than those of her youth. It was a Sabbath without a father, without a rabbi, with little order or law. It was a quiet sunset, Vermont Sabbath of shared murmurings and delicate tastings.

Once we had gone together to see Shlomo Carlebach, a famous Hebrew folksinger, and I cried. I remember thinking it odd that I should cry. How strange it felt to be moved in such a way. But I cried because he touched something in me, made me feel something I'd either forgotten or never had felt; *me*, a non-Jewish Jew, even a Jewish goy. I remembered marching for Israel's Bar Mitzvah when I was twelve and somebody put a flag in my Sunday school hand and told me to march. I obeyed, never thinking of it, never questioning it, until many years later when I felt hopelessly confused.

And now I was at my cousin's engagement party. Damn that party. It was the early 1970s, a time of social unrest, and I had vowed not to engage these people in political discussion and had even said so to a girl I'd met on the train.

"Oh, are you Jewish?" she'd asked.

"Well, *half*. My mother's Jewish."

"Doesn't that make you Jewish?" she'd said. "Israel would take you in, wouldn't it?"

Arriving at the party, the first person I'd seen was Aunt Claire, rich-looking and cool, glamorous even with her gray-streaked hair, lounging about on the couch smoking cigarettes from a holder. Uncle Joe scurried about the kitchen wearing an apron, assisting the caterer, issuing instructions in his weird Polish accent. At last he came out, untying his apron.

"Well Joe," Aunt Claire said. "Finished in the kitchen? Sid down. Enjoy yourself. Eat some strudel."

"I tell you, these caterers," he said. "Take your eyes off them a minute and they go cuckoo." He shed the apron and walked over to the couch. Several guests had already arrived, mostly friends of Claire's and Joe's. Cousin Erwin was somewhere downstairs with his fiancé.

I had never been close to these people. Aunt Claire was the younger society version of my mother, almost identical in appearance, but in personality as different as could be. As long as I could remember, there'd been a rivalry between the two. According to my mother, it existed even when they were children in Germany. Once in the early `50s, Claire and Erwin had flown out from Philadelphia to visit us in California. The visit lasted exactly three days, ending abruptly when Claire scooped little Erwin up one evening and hastily departed. The official explanation was that we'd all been innocently listening to the radio when I, in the full glory of my five years, stood up on the table and announced that the radio was mine and Erwin was not to listen to it, whereupon Claire became hysterical.

It always amazed me, though, how–being the only Holocaust survivors of a large family–my mother and her sister could still hate each other so. For years during World War II, they'd been separated. It was only later in America that they'd found each through the Red Cross, on opposite ends of the continent, and had their reunion. The first week, I'm told, was all hugs and tears; then the fighting recommenced. The world war, it seemed, had interrupted a private war and when the big one ended, the smaller one resumed.

For the rest of my life, though, I shall never forget the look of the tattoo on Aunt Claire's arm, nor will I forget the first time I saw it. I think it was during that visit to California in `54. One night at dinner she leaned over and the sleeve of her dress slid up, revealing a forearm. There, in angry blue ink that seemed to be melting, a five-digit number glared up as if daring me to comment. I didn't say a word, but Aunt Claire must have seen me staring because she quickly straightened herself up, pushing the delinquent sleeve back down over her arm.

Later I asked my mother about it. She wouldn't say much, only that Aunt Claire had been held prisoner by some bad men who had drawn on her arm and caused her much pain.

"Do you have a tattoo, mommy?" I'd asked.

"No," she said, "because mommy got away from the bad men to a place called China where there were *other* bad men, but they didn't draw numbers on people's arms."

We never spoke of Aunt Claire's tattoo again, and I never saw it again either, except occasionally behind closed eyelids. But over the years the image of those numbers grew in my mind, assumed greater proportion and significance, until finally I couldn't think of Aunt Claire without seeing that tattoo.

I was thinking of it now, in fact, as I sat in the living room of her house in Philadelphia. "Sometimes you think it's better to do it yourself," Uncle Joe was saying, still berating the caterers.

"No complaints," Aunt Claire insisted, shushing him. "Sid down and be with your guests, they wanna see you."

"Yes, *siddown* Joe," said a lady next to me. "We come to your house; the least you can be is *here!*"

Grumbling good naturedly, Joe sat down on the couch and allowed his wife to pour him a drink. "Now, *this*-this is good service," he said. "I can't complain. Tell me, Friedel, have you met my nephew from California? Such a fine-looking young man, and vid long hair."

"Have a piece of strudel," she said, reaching for a knife.

"No thank you," I said.

"What's a matter?" she said, "your aunt's strudel ain't good enough for you? You're a growing boy, you need to eat."

"Not a boy," Aunt Claire corrected, "he's a *man*."

"Ah, excuse me," Friedel said, "a growing *man*. So whadaya do, growing man, go to school?"

"Well, not exactly," I muttered, my mouth full of the strudel which, naturally, had been crammed onto my plate despite my protests.

"Not exactly?" inquired Uncle Joe. "Vat, not exactly?" He turned to Aunt Claire. "Not exactly," he says. He turned back to me. "So, vat *exactly* do you do?"

"I study, but not at a school," I said, choosing my words carefully. "I live in New York now, and study on my own."

"And what good does that do?" Friedel wanted to know. "Will it get you a job?"

"I've taken some time off from school," I said, "but it's not forever."

"And what does your mother think of this?" chimed in Uncle Joe.

"She's ok with it," I lied. "I'll be going back soon."

"That's vat dey *all* say," said Uncle Joe, winking at Friedel.

"Leave him alone, Joe," Aunt Claire said.

"Vat did I say?" Uncle Joe answered, feigning puzzlement.

A swarm of new guests arrived, and the room dissipated into a hodgepodge of impressions; empty wine glasses, filled ones, mirrors, paintings, fur coats, silly hairdos, lipstick.

It was a chance for me to escape. I excused myself and went to the bathroom. It was the biggest bathroom I'd ever seen. Thick, plush purple fur covered the toilet seat. I ran the fingers of my right hand over it, while flushing the toilet with my left. I watched the water swirl 'round and 'round before stepping back into the hallway.

Knickknacks from Israel covered its walls. I took my time, scrutinizing each one. There was an old photograph of Uncle Joe and Aunt Claire standing by what I took to be the Wailing Wall. And a small scroll inscribed in Hebrew next to a larger Star of David that looked golden and gaudy. I glanced over my shoulder and saw Friedel eyeing me through the half-open doorway to the hall.

"You were looking at the things from Israel?" she observed. "Have you been there yet?"

"Not yet," I confessed.

"Friends," Uncle Joe said as I re-entered the living room. "My nephew from California. He's living in New York now, where he doesn't exactly go to school."

"Do you *believe* in Israel?" Friedel asked suddenly. It was the question I'd been dreading since first walking through their front door.

"Oh, for heaven's sake," Claire said, "let's not talk about politics. This is an engagement party."

"Shush," Joe said, "I vanna hear his answer."

The entire room grew silent. This was not only the moment I'd dreaded, but the moment I'd dreaded on steroids. "It's a party," Claire repeated, suddenly less sure of herself.

"Will you be quiet now?" Joe insisted. "My nephew is asked a question and I vant to hear his answer. It's a fine young man ve have here and vit long hair. Ven else can ve hear vat da younger generation is thinking?" Then, turning to me, he said, "Please answer the question."

There would be no more escapes, at least not today. I cleared my throat. "Actually," I began tentatively, "my feelings about Israel are mixed."

"Mixed?" he shot back. "Whada hell does that mean, *mixed*? Either you're vit Israel or you're not."

"Well, for me it's more complicated than that," I offered.

"What's complicated?" Joe said.

Claire abruptly got up and sauntered towards the kitchen. "Listen," she said, "I got better things to do today than listen to political discussions at my son's engagement party."

"Be quiet," Friedel said, "I wanna hear what he has to say." Claire shut the door to the kitchen and was gone.

"The point is," I ventured, "that there are two sides to the thing. I think we have to ask ourselves what the other side wants."

"Vants?" shot Joe. "Who gives a damn what they vant?"

"*I* do," I said, and already I could feel the faint but rising tide of madness tickling the insides of my belly, but I fought it, didn't give in to it, not just yet anyway.

There were murmurs of disapproval from everyone, then silence.

"You mean you support the Arabs?" Joe asked, more as an accusation than a question. I felt like laughing but didn't. Maybe I should have.

"I didn't say that."

"You said you care about them."

"And I do," I assured him. "Just as I care about *all* human beings."

"People who kill women and children aren't human beings." This from a man seated on the couch across the room.

"The Jews do that!" I snapped and immediately regretted it.

"Oh, so now the Jews aren't human beings?" Joe inquired.

"I didn't say that."

"I know exactly vat you said," he countered, "do you think I'm stupid? You think Jews are stupid?"

I struggled hard for composure. I took a deep breath and counted to five. "What I mean is this," I continued as calmly as I could. "*Both* sides kill women and children because there's a war going on and that's what happens in war. We can go on matching atrocities and end up exactly where we started. Or we can ask ourselves what the fight's about to begin with and recognize that there is some validity to the claims of both sides. We will solve nothing until we stop looking at it as Jews and Arabs and start looking at it as human beings; we've got to see both sides, otherwise we're lost."

It was an excellent speech. I stopped to catch my breath amid the general silence. For a moment, I thought maybe I'd swayed them, but then the voice from across the room thundered back to life like a goddamned loudspeaker.

"As long as I live," the man on the couch said, "Israel will not be overrun. I will die fighting on Jewish soil rather than live to see it taken from us. If you love Arabs so much, go to Russia."

And that's when I lost it. "But I *don't* love Arabs," I protested, "any more than I love non-Arabs. And I *certainly* don't love the Russians. You haven't been listening at all!"

"Please, Joe." It was Claire, speaking from the now-open door to the kitchen. She was looking directly at him, as if he were the only person in the room. She spoke calmly, but with obvious effort. "It's your son's engagement party. Don't ruin it."

"Oh, vir just having a little *poleedical* discussion," Joe said. "Go back in the kitchen. Your nephew just said he don't like Jews any more than he likes Arabs."

"That's not..." I started, but Joe drowned me out.

"That's exactly vat you said! If ve had a tape recorder, I would play you da tape."

"Oh, Christ."

"Don't curse," Joe said. "Curse vit your Marxist friends, not in this house. This is a Jewish house."

He opened the jeweled box on the coffee table, withdrew a cigar, lit it, and began angrily puffing. He stared impassively at the wall opposite him, and I could see the veins swelling up in his neck. "Listen," he said, stuffing the cigar into an ashtray. "I'm gonna tell you something. Don't think your Marxist friends let you in; don't think you're one of them. To them you're a Jew, no matter vat you think. After the revolution, they'll turn on you, mark my words."

"Marx was a Jew," I said.

"Scratch a *goy,* you gotta fascist," he said, as if I hadn't spoken at all.

"Shut up now!" screamed Claire from the kitchen. "I don't want to hear another word. So, your nephew's a communist, are you happy?"

"He's a *radical,*" Joe observed wryly, retrieving his cigar.

"I don't want to hear it!" Claire screamed. "His ancestors were killed by radicals; I don't want to hear about *radicals*."

"That's not what I'm talking about," I protested, by now rather weakly.

"Maybe you *should*," said Joe, sitting straight up on the edge of the couch and pointing his cigar at me like the finger of that long-ago ghostly Jew praying white-faced in the synagogue. "Lemme tell you a story. Ven I was your age, I was vit Russia. You vanna know how they treat Jews? Ven I was a young man I was vit Russia, and they came for me, anyway. They took me into a little room and a man sat down and pudda pistol on the table and said, 'now you gonna tell us vat ve vanna know or you get a bullet in the head.' That's how the Marxists treat Jews."

"It was wartime," I said.

He looked at me and for the first time I could see the darkness in his soul, the anguish streaming from his eyes in terse, staccato bursts. "The war never ended," he said. He put the cigar back in his mouth, took a puff and blew it toward the ceiling.

The sting of that smoke burns my eyes still.

THE INITIATION

In the fall of `69, when Gordon Davis entered Goddard College as a freshman, he was nothing more than a gangly kid from Nebraska with a burning desire to be avant-garde. Two years later, he was a lot less gangly.

This was doubtless due to the fatty foods he'd been consuming in the cafeteria, the only outlet available for nourishment on this tiny campus in the green hills of central Vermont. But on the crisp, chilly morning in question, food was the last thing on Gordon's mind. For this, he knew, was the day he would have to decide.

Though it seemed like years, it had been only months since he'd first heard of what promised to be the most massive anti-war protest in American history. Gordon hadn't conceived the plan; that had been done by accomplished men and women with famous and feared names in Los Angeles, Boston, and

53

New York-people often mentioned in the pages of *Ramparts* and the *Berkeley BARB*. Gordon was decidedly not one of those people. And yet, he sometimes felt as if the idea had been *his*.

That's why he'd been ill-prepared for what Danny Lopez had said to him just a week ago today. "The thing is," he'd said, "there could be violence. Some protestors will be packing guns. They'll be looking for a fight; it's probably gonna be a bloodbath."

Danny's source for this information was his older brother, Jaime, who was a leader in the Brown Berets–an organization of Hispanic radicals–and therefore ostensibly in a position to know such things. And the particular protestors he was talking about, Gordon knew, were unpredictable; a newly minted group that had recently announced its intention to spark the second American Revolution by any means necessary.

"Are you sure?" Gordon had asked on the steps of Conrad Hall as his breath dissipated in the steam of a chilly Vermont morning.

"Let me put it this way, bro," Danny had said, eying his friend with the amused condescension that so often characterized the attitude of oppressed minorities toward their less-enlightened white brethren. "The Puerto Ricans may not go; we feel that it could be strategically dangerous..."

Gordon was familiar with the dismissive attitude. Danny, in fact, *hailed* from Puerto Rico and never tired of reminding his more mundane comrades of that fortuitous fact. He always wore a black beret riddled with tiny red pins bearing slogans in angry Spanish and, for at least the past year, had been carefully cultivating a neat black goatee. The resemblance to Che Guevara was striking.

"Are you *sure?*" Gordon repeated, never doubting for a minute that he was.

"Just don't claim that I didn't warn you," Danny said, and with that he walked out the door.

For Gordon, the incident had been as annoying as it was typical. But he couldn't dismiss it outright; there probably was something to what his black-bearded friend had said. Hence, the dilemma: to go or not to go?

On the surface, the plan seemed straight forward; gather thousands of protestors in the Capital Mall for a genuine show of support. The idea, Gordon understood, was to show that opposition to the Vietnam War was no longer marginal; that it had, in fact, become mainstream. The protest would be huge and nonviolent. Fed by buses from the entire East Coast, it would be meticulously planned and masterfully executed. With any luck, in fact, it would mark a historic turning point in the ongoing struggle for peace.

But now an unholy worm was writhing in the otherwise enticing jam of the upcoming protest; what if it wasn't nonviolent at all? What if, as Danny suggested, a large contingent of demonstrators showed up with an entirely different agenda?

The result, Gordon knew, could be catastrophic; not only for the movement but for those individuals whose lives it would put on the line. And yet, as the appointed bus monitor for central Vermont, he had made a promise. It was actually *more* than a promise; to bow out now, he knew, would be humiliating.

On the morning before the demonstration, Gordon awoke with the sun. The drive to Washington, D.C. would take most of the day, and if he were going to do this thing, they would have to get started early. He rolled over in bed and stared at the clock. Yes, he thought, this was the day he would have to decide; it was now or never.

Reluctantly he got out of bed, shuffled to the sink, and stared into the mirror above it. What he saw there didn't surprise him; except for the details, in fact, it was not unlike what he'd been seeing for nearly two years. It was the face of a young man with blond hair down to his shoulders and a dazed look in his eyes. The look was familiar, he'd seen it everywhere; on the faces of classmates, on Danny's face, even on the faces of the violent radicals whose motives he now feared. Yes, on their faces *especially* he'd seen that look.

Once he'd gone to see a psychiatrist in New York City. It was during a hard time when his girlfriend had left him, and he felt completely confused. The shrink had taken one look at him and commented, "I can tell a lot just from looking at person's face."

"Oh," Gordon had said casually, "and what can you tell from looking at *mine*?"

"I see a lot of pain," the guy had said without a moment's hesitation.

Long after that brief therapy had ended, long after he'd forgotten all about the girlfriend and gone on with his life, the comment had stuck in Gordon's mind. At moments like this, it came back to haunt him.

Suddenly there was a knock on the door. Gordon dabbed some water on his face, gargled, threw a robe over his naked frame, and greeted Danny. Without a word, the dark-haired Puerto Rican sauntered into the room and sat down on the bed. "What's up?" he said. Gordon sat down next to him. "So, today's the big day, eh?" Danny said.

Gordon shrugged. "What's the latest on the radicals?" he asked.

Danny just sat there looking like the bearer of unwelcome news. It was the first time in months that Gordon had seen him without the characteristic smirk. "It's definite," Danny said, "the situation is way too unstable; we're staying home."

Gordon glanced to his right in the mirror's direction. He wanted to see himself in that mirror again, wanted to capture another glimpse of that bewildered look. It was a doomed look of dull terror offering proof of his utter confusion. But the door upon which the mirror hung stood closed, hiding his image in the closet. And so Gordon knew he would have to proceed without the help of a self-reflection.

"Let's just hope you're wrong," he said.

Danny didn't look surprised. He seemed to observe the scene from a distance for a second, then quickly reached into a coat pocket and pulled something out. "If you're really going," he said, "take this with you." At first Gordon couldn't see what it was, then he could; a small revolver. The scene reminded him of a TV show he used to watch as a kid. "No thanks," Gordon said.

Danny looked at him as if he weren't there, and suddenly it occurred to Gordon that this was no TV show at all but real life, and that the gun was no toy. It wasn't often that he'd been this close to one. He looked at it with curiosity, then growing discomfort. A gun outside a display case was like a captured wild animal outside its cage; both could bite. He could no more put something like that in his pocket than he would a poisonous snake.

Gordon swallowed, trying hard to control the crazy writhing that seemed to have begun in his throat. "I'm taking a wet wash rag in case of tear gas and that's it," he said.

Danny grunted and shoved the gun back into his pocket. For the first time in a week, Gordon felt a pang of relief. "Hope you know what you're doing, man," Danny said.

The ride to Washington passed quickly. Because Gordon was a coordinator, he got to ride up front with a clipboard on his lap bearing the names of all those on board. It was his responsibility to make sure everybody got there and, more importantly, got back. He was sitting next to a woman named Diane Goldberg, a wild-eyed neurotic who had borrowed thousands of dollars from the government for her education, utterly convinced the coming revolution would save her from ever having to pay it back. As they approached Washington late in the day, she gave Gordon a nudge. "Give a little speech, Gordy" she urged. "Tell 'em what to expect."

So he stood up, thought for a moment, and said, "Stick together, brothers and sisters. If the shit hits the fan, take care of each other." It was all he could think of, and it was ridiculous. He sat down, embarrassed, with an image of Danny in the back of his mind.

They arrived just before dark. The Student Mobilization Committee had arranged for the use of an enormous church in which demonstrators could pitch their sleeping bags; to Gordon it looked like a gala campout of the kind he'd attended many times as a young Boy Scout. Only here, the uniform was different: long hair, jeans pocked with holes, and, he couldn't help but notice, the same blank stare with which he had become so familiar. As the campers prepared for the night, there was a spirit of jubilance and celebration, but to Gordon it seemed forced.

He hit the sack early but got very little sleep. Around 5 a.m. people started rolling out of their sleeping bags. He did too, and then joined the grim line of protestors filing silently through the pre-dawn light to where the march would begin. It occurred to him they were like soldiers marching to combat in the darkness, impressed with the seriousness of what they were about to undertake.

Some wore silver helmets; many wore armbands of red and black with military fatigue jackets bearing various slogans. There was something happening here; Gordon could sense it but couldn't quite grasp what it was, something beyond the vacuous stares they shared. It was something stronger and more durable. As he trudged along with a growling stomach, he tried to focus on just what it was, but could catch only glimpses. The body of the thing seemed to be crouching behind buildings, mixed with the sunrise, barely visible yet still determined to receive its full due.

In the chilly morning air, student marshals stood posted every fifty feet, mostly youthful men and women with overlong hair and blank looks much like Gordon's. They too wore helmets and red armbands as they barked instructions. "Keep moving," they grunted, "don't stop."

The line of protestors curled like a snake as far as the eye could see.

The route of the march was well-planned, Gordon observed. It looped in a wide circle, gradually zeroing in on the Washington Monument where later, Gordon had been told, there would be a rally.

All along the route, yellow roadblocks on either side barred automobile traffic from the area. Stationed at intervals along the way, groups of policemen huddled in their uniforms, somber and unsmiling. At one point the march passed what appeared to be a Catholic girl's school; an aging ivy-covered affair with a large courtyard enclosed by a wall. The only entrance seemed to be the front gate, a huge wrought-iron monstrosity behind which a large silent company of National Guardsmen crouched at grim khaki-clad attention. With rifles gleaming and bayonets fixed, they seemed ready to pounce on the demonstrators and rip out their guts. In the morning darkness, they looked like ghosts.

As the march wore on, Gordon began observing his fellow marchers more closely. He noticed cliques among the demonstrators; small groups bearing strange flags chanting their own private slogans. He wondered where those much-feared radicals were; did they have a flag too or had they mmersed themselves in the crowd, awaiting the right moment to pounce?

Yet somehow, his earlier fears now seemed exaggerated. Lord, what a concoction of humanity had turned out today; he'd had no idea that such a warm swarm of people stood against the war. Amid all this, the radicals seemed like just another small faction with its own peculiar brand of revolution. Such groups, it occurred to him, should be pitied rather than feared. He began to relax, feeling that even those radicals were his brothers.

Then the trouble started. It was late afternoon after most of the marchers had already arrived at the monument and were waiting patiently on the grass for the rally to begin. Gordon had just entered the home stretch, his feet aching with blisters, when he noticed the commotion at an immense government building nearby. By the time he got there a small crowd had gathered and, behind it, a confused line of police.

"What's going on?" Gordon asked a short kid with glasses, who answered with a shrug.

"Somebody pulled down the American flag and put up a North Vietnamese one," he said.

Gordon moved up as close as he could to the police line, staring over uniformed shoulders to see what was going on. Something was happening; people were running around yelling into the wind. He couldn't see the subversive flag, but the thought of it stirred a strange excitement in him; a hint of triumph, to be sure, but also an unnerving fear, something tugging at him like a flapping clothesline tied to the end of his lower intestine.

Suddenly there was a clamor from behind, and he turned just in time to see some fifty helmeted figures wearing fatigue jackets and red armbands marching in his direction with seemingly grim determination. "Ho-Ho-Ho Chi Minh," they chanted in unison, "dare to struggle, dare to win!"

He glanced over his shoulder and saw that the police too had turned. He watched, fascinated, as they slipped on their gas masks and raised their clubs, then realized he was standing between the police line and its chanting foes. Great, he thought, I'll be the first to get shot. Shaking off his paralysis, he raced to the side of the street and up the steps of a sizeable building only to be stopped by its locked double doors. Trapped, he pressed his nose into the crack between the doors, holding his breath to see what would happen.

Behind him in the streets, a strange popping began. Was it gun fire, had the radicals brought their weapons after all? He pressed himself hard against the doors, pushing into them for dear life as if trying to penetrate solid matter like a character in some science fiction epic. But it didn't happen; with a sinking heart, he realized he was there for the duration. Then something hit the wall above him and bounced off, landing on the steps. It gave off a loud hissing sound as his eyes began to water. "You motherfuckers!" he heard somebody yell and knew instinctively it was a cop.

Gordon could barely breathe. Each time he inhaled, his nose and throat stung horribly, and his eyes felt like somebody had poured acid into them. He pulled the wet washcloth out of his coat pocket and dabbed his face with it. It helped a little, but not very much.

He tried to think of Vietnam, but all he could see was blackness. Somewhere in that blackness were dead women and children and burning villages and napalmed babies. He knew they were there, but he couldn't make them out. It was too dark, too noisy; *my God*, he thought, *what am I doing here?* And for perhaps the first time in his life, he felt real fear.

But as quickly as it started, the panic passed. For a time Gordon didn't move, not trusting it was safe. When he finally turned around, the street was nearly silent. Yet, off in the distance he could still hear the stirrings of chaos. His eyes, nose and throat were a mass of watery pain and he was nearly blind.

He took off his tee shirt, tore it down the middle and tied it to his right arm in his own version of a white flag, the universal sign of surrender. Then, feeling his way along the sides of the building, he slowly made his way out, heading painfully towards the long-waiting bus. Years later, remembering the March on Washington, the image that would come to mind was the one of that morning; a grim line of determined demonstrators marching out into darkness to do battle. They were the antiwar warriors and the long-haired hippie freaks. They were the generation that would change America.

And they *were* a generation; perhaps for the first time, Gordon really understood that as he felt his way along those broad empty walls. They were girls and boys, college students, future parents. But underneath their dazed eyes, they'd been glowing that morning and only *they* had seen the glow. They could recognize each other anywhere; they would *always* recognize each other. And somehow Gordon knew that he was exactly where he should be.

As he crossed the grim line of gas-masked policemen encircling the area, one of them wordlessly raised a camera and snapped his picture. The light of the flash careened like a rainbow back and forth in the water of his eyes, and Gordon remembered–only yesterday–frantically searching an unfriendly mirror for even the hint of a blurry self-image. Perhaps, it occurred to him now, this policeman's photo was the only self-image he would ever need. For today he had crossed the threshold from invisibility to recognition. Today, Gordon reflected, he had finally been seen.

Parting like the Red Sea, the line of police officers allowed him to pass. Just a little further, Gordon thought, and the world would be new.

THE TORTOISE AND THE HAIR

This is a story about the end of an era. It was 1975, and I'd been hearing rumors for months but refused to believe them. My mother would call me and, after a long insidious conversation, casually remark; "Well, dear, how's your hair looking?"

"Same as always, Mom," I'd say, already sensing where the conversation was headed.

"Oh?" she'd say, punctuating her question with a pregnant pause. "That's odd; I heard that you hippies were cutting your hair."

"Where'd you hear that, Mom?"

"Everywhere." Another pause, then; "You know, son, styles change. It's not 1967 anymore."

"Thank God for that."

"Women like a man's hair to be neat now. I'm not saying you should *cut* it, understand. I just think you should know a woman's point of view."

"Yeah," I'd mutter. "Well, thanks, Mom."

Another pregnant pause.

"You know," she'd go on, "there's a place that does custom cuts for just ten dollars. They're experts; they know what looks good on different heads. I heard it in the news; the announcer said they were doing great business with young people. I'm not saying you should *go*, don't misunderstand. I just think it's interesting, don't you?"

"How's Dad?" I'd put in.

"You want me to send you the money, dear? I'll pay for it."

"No. Thanks, but that's ok."

"Really, son, it's no trouble. I *want* to do it. I think you should look nice, don't you? It's the least a mother can do."

"No, Mom."

"Please don't take this little thing away from me," she'd plead, sounding as if she were near tears. "Really, I *want* to do it. I'll put a check in tomorrow's mail."

"For Crissakes, Mom..."

"Don't talk that way to your mother, David. It hurts when you talk like that."

And three days later I'd receive a check in the mail that I would promptly deposit and forget. Only I kept noticing hair. It's a strange thing, the way hair consciousness works; it creeps up on you like taxes. One day you're a carefree youthful man, and the next? Well, the next day you're glancing nervously at the reflection of your shoulder-length blond hair in every store window you pass.

Then came the clincher. I was sitting in a café one day when Jan, an old friend, walked in. Jan was an attractive redhead with fantastic blue eyes, one of those sophisticated types who's lived in Europe and speaks a gazillion languages. I motioned her over to my table and asked how she was.

She ran both hands over her thighs smoothing her skirt, sat down, smiled at me and, placing her fingers on the table, leaned forward to confront me with those shocking blue eyes. "I'm great," she said, "how are *you*?"

"Not sure," I confided. "My mom thinks I should cut my hair."

"Oh *do*," she said, without a nanosecond's hesitation.

I stared at her. "I don't mean to be impolite," Jan went on, "but, well, men have been getting sloppy lately. It's not the `60s anymore, David. The time of the hippies has flown. I think a good haircut would look great on you."

That clinched it. I still put up a brief resistance, but it was merely symbolic; Jan knew it, I knew it, even my *mother* knew it. I was defeated.

The man who performed the procedure was a friend of Jan's; someone, she assured me, who could be trusted. For weeks before the appointment, I tried not to think of what I was about to endure. It seemed almost impossible.

On the day of the procedure, I woke up early and had a light breakfast. I was feeling a little queasy and had to forgo my coffee. The drive to the salon seemed interminable. As I walked up the front steps, I felt faint and the world swam before me in a blaze of colors. I stopped and leaned on the railing, feeling sick. The sign on the door undulated before me like a worn-out hula dancer.

But Jan was with me, acting as my rock. She took my arm and gently whispered into my ear. "There's no turning back now, David. You need to be brave." And so it came to pass that one of the last surviving hippies in America took a deep breath, squared his slovenly shoulders, and marched squarely through that door.

Here's the thing: The person who walked in that day, never walked out.

Part II
SPACE

THE ORANGE JAR

He said he'd been a revolutionary. He used to tell stories about all the things he'd done. The children, seated at his knees on the rug, would fold their hands patiently and wait for him to begin.

"I used to be a revolutionary," he'd say wild-eyed, like a preacher on a bridge. "I was against all war. We used to surround government buildings to exorcise their evil spirits. Our leaders told us if we chanted loud enough, we could raise them off the ground and all the devils would come tumbling right out. Then we could chase those petty demons with sticks and anyone fast enough could catch one and bring him home."

He'd pause long enough for this to sink in as the children's eyes turned wide. Then he'd continue.

"I was a young man then," he'd say through his snarled gray beard. "I could run fast and caught me an excellent one. Now I keep him locked up in the top drawer of my dresser, would you like to see?"

And before anyone could object, he'd be on his feet, quickly closing the distance between himself and the top dresser door. The children would gasp. Too apprehensive to speak, they would sit with their little mouths gaping and their breath coming out in short wispy bursts.

Arriving at the dresser, the old man would turn and, noticing the agitated state of his audience, seek to reassure them. "Don't worry, kids," he'd say, "I keep him in a jar. It's tightly shut; very difficult for him to escape, have no fear."

Then he'd turn dramatically back toward the dresser, open the drawer with a flourish and, amid the nervous rustling of the children, withdraw a small container and place it carefully on the coffee table in the middle of the brightly lit room. The sides of the jar had been painted a vivid orange, making it impossible to see inside.

"It used to be clear," he'd explain, "but that was way too dangerous. People would tease him and get him all worked up until he tried to get out. Once he almost broke the glass and got away. That's when I painted it. He hasn't given me too much trouble in a while. Lately, though, he's been thumping in the night, which worries me a bit."

To the children's horror, the old man would pick up the jar and give it a vigorous shake. "Hey little devil," he'd say, "are you getting restless in there? You want out?"

Then he'd pause while the children held their breaths. But nothing ever happened. So, finally, the old man would place the jar back on the table with a sigh. "I guess not today," he'd say. "He's probably resting up."

Occasionally at this point his presentation would be interrupted by a barely audible shriek from somewhere in the hallway outside. But the old man would just shrug and continue with his stories.

Like the time he'd gone to Chicago for a big national protest. How he'd seen a cop push a pregnant woman through a window, leaving blood everywhere. How she'd just laid there screaming while the police stood around and laughed.

That's when the children's teacher would usually interrupt by clearing her throat. "It all happened a very long time ago," she'd assure them, assuming a light tone for the children but a stern look for the narrator. "Nothing like that will ever happen to any of *you*."

So he'd go on. Later, he'd say, there was an even bigger demonstration in Washington. He and several others had thrown rocks at the soldiers, who'd hit them back with billy clubs and put them in jail. His cell smelled like a sewer. He'd spent five days with blood on his face and very little food before finally being allowed to see a doctor.

The old man would glance around, often noticing blank expressions on the faces of his listeners. They never seemed bored, just uncomprehending. So he'd try even harder.

"I had a friend once," he'd say. "I met him in prison, and we were very close. We used to talk about everything; our parents, women, ideas, politics. They got him later in a riot. Said he was a ringleader. The coroner said he'd been shot seven times."

The teacher was about to speak up again when she was interrupted by a rap on the door. Without waiting for a reply, a youthful woman wearing blue scrubs stepped into the room and smiled. "Visitation is over," she said. "Time for the children to leave."

The teacher looked relieved.

Silently–almost reverently–they gathered their things together. The old man saw he was about to lose his audience and felt distressed. He badly needed to make an impression; sorely wanted them to remember this day.

Startling the children with his suddenness, he picked up the orange jar that by now sat almost forgotten on the coffee table and held it up before his audience.

"This is all the revolution I need now," he said. "Here are my spoils, this is my reward. I have the devil in the palm of my hand. I have the devil locked up and guard him with my life. As long as this jar remains sealed, everything will be just fine."

A slight drop of saliva appeared at the corner of the old man's mouth and slowly dribbled down his chin. Then the teacher hustled the children out the door and led them through wide empty halls to the bus outside, where they soon found themselves en route back to their classroom to spend the afternoon discussing their visit to a mental hospital.

Years later when the old man died, one of the psychiatric aides, going through his things, found the little orange jar snuggled neatly between two shirts in his top dresser drawer. She was about to throw it out when, remembering that it was his prize possession, she felt a sudden fondness for him and took it home. There she placed it on the long mantle above her fireplace.

Often, when company comes, someone will comment on the strange little orange jar on the mantle and ask what it is. When that happens, the aide always laughs, makes a joke of it, and quickly changes the subject.

The truth is, she's afraid one day someone might ask to have a look inside.

THE GOOD SAMARITAN

If it'd been me, I'd have stopped. The fact is, I stopped anyway, even though it wasn't me. I guess some people have no compassion.

It happened a few years ago, right after Christmas. I'd been down to my aunt's in Philadelphia and was driving home up old Vermont State Route 100 around 1 a.m. when I saw it. I'd been nodding off a bit and kind of worried about getting pulled over, or worse, ending up in a ditch. The truth is I'd had a few nips of Bourbon and you know how dark it can get along old Route 100.

Anyway, I was cruising along minding my own business, listening to *Bye Bye Miss American Pie* on the AM, keeping a respectable distance from the guy in front of me, staring at his taillights, when suddenly he swerved and went over a bump. Something shot out from under his back bumper; a squirming gray thing that, in the gleam of my headlights, looked like a sparkling silver fish struggling on the tip of a spear. Except there wasn't any ocean, and this was definitely no spear. In fact, it was a cat.

I swerved too, to avoid running over him again, and felt sure the guy in front would stop to see what he'd done. But, as I say, some people don't have a conscience. Well, thank God there was at least *one* good Samaritan on the road that night; I pulled over, got my flashlight out of the glove compartment, and walked over to where the animal lay kicking on the pavement.

He was big. *Real* big. He looked like he was probably handsome once too. But he wasn't handsome anymore; his whole hind end lay crushed and stuck to the pavement like papier mâché matting, while the front of him–the half that was alive–just kept kicking wildly, trying to get the back half unstuck. "Oh, my goodness!" I said to him, lighting his panicked yellow eyes up with my flashlight. "Looks like you pretty well messed yourself up. Guess that'll teach you not to cross the road at night."

I was considering how to put him out of his misery when a diesel truck rolled up and a thin man wearing faded Levi's and a cowboy shirt hopped out of the cab and sauntered towards me. "What's up?" he growled, puffing on a stogie.

I shifted the gaze of my flashlight to get a better look at the newcomer. He was in his late twenties and spoke with a Southern accent, maybe Texan. "Poor cat got splattered all over the road," I said, noticing a black scar on the stranger's cheek the size of a crater.

"Ran out in front of you?" he asked.

"Not me," I said, "but I don't think I can help him."

He yanked the stogie out of his mouth and flipped it onto the road. "Better finish him," the maybe-Texan said. "I gotta pistol in the truck." The embers of his cigar bounced twice on the pavement and lay there like so many dead fireflies. Before he could say any more, a big-ass Oldsmobile pulled up and a male voice that sounded like velvet pin cushions asked what was going on.

"Cat's been hit," I said, "and it looks pretty bad." I turned my light on the driver.

"Really?" said the man in the Olds, opening his door. Probably in his mid-fifties, he was as fat as a beach ball and sporting a tux. "My goodness, that's dreadful!" he said with a placid expression on his face belying his words. The gargantuan man was trying to get out of the car, but it looked like the effort was enervating. "Did you hear that, Emma? A cat's been hit, isn't that terrible?"

The Texan shrugged and squatted on his haunches.

"Awful," said Emma, opening the door on the other side. She was almost, though not quite, as fat as her husband and wearing a sparkling red dress. "I won't be able to look at it, George," she said, stepping around the front of the car. Taking George by the arm, she yanked him out of the driver's seat and casually guided him towards us.

For about five seconds we all watched, fascinated by the squirming thing on the road.

"Gonna finish him," the Texan grunted. "Gotta pistol in my rig."

The enormous cat let loose a giant kick with his front leg, and I thought I heard it snap. Then came a pitiful cry, but not from the cat. "A pistol?" shrieked Emma. "You're not gonna fire off a gun here, young man! Tell 'em, George."

George glanced sheepishly around the circle. "Emma doesn't like guns," he confirmed. Then, turning to her: "It does seem like the most efficacious thing to do, my dear."

"George, that's ghastly!" she objected. "The very thought of it chills my blood. I'm warning you, if this young man as much as shows that weapon, I'll get into the car and drive on alone. I mean it, George!"

George smiled meekly at the Texan, then at me. "Emma doesn't like guns," he repeated, wiping his palms off on his pant legs.

"Sheesh!" said the Texan, spitting on the pavement. But he just went on squatting, staring into space as if lost in thought.

The bickering was getting to me. If there's one thing I hate, it's indecision. Suddenly I thought of a solution. "Why not run him over?" I suggested. "That'll do the job for sure."

No one said anything for a minute. Then the squatting Texan struggled to his feet, sauntered to the truck, hopped into its cab, and started the engine. "We'll need more light," George said. He waddled over to his car and returned with a giant, expensive-looking flashlight.

So, there we were, Mr. and Mrs. Tux and yours truly, shining the light on the doomed cat, watching him squirm. Suddenly the enormous truck jerked to life, rumbled forward, and stopped just short of the cat. The animal lay bathed in the truck's headlights, making the blood on its fur shine like Red Mountain Wine. "Hold it steady, friend," I instructed George, taking hold of one of his wrists with my free hand to make sure he was doing it right.

The old cat just stared back at us, his eyes blazing like lumps of charcoal after the flame's gone down.

The Texan leaned out of his cab and looked at the cat for a second to make sure his aim was true. Then he gunned the engine, and the truck lurched forward. The first time he ran over the part already stuck to the pavement and the old cat just started squirming and hollering more frantically than ever, so the Texan backed up for a second try. He ran over the middle and I saw it go flat under his wheel as the old cat's eyes bulged like nothing I'd ever seen before and he opened his mouth to let out a howl, but a pile of guts came shooting out instead. We did him again for good measure, and this time we ran over the head, squashing it like a ripe tomato, and I could hear the enormous animal's skull crack, spilling his brains all over the pavement.

We did him three more times and after we'd finished, he was nothing but a cat rug. As we stood basking in the warmth of our good deed, a single thought kept running through my head. I said it before, and I'll say it again; thank God there was at least *one* good Samaritan on the road that night.

SOCIAL JUSTICE

I picked him up at the corner of Seventh Avenue and Fourteenth Street. He said he wanted to go to the Upper East Side, so I turned left. It was a busy night with lots of traffic; I was lucky to get him into my cab. He was in a hurry, he said, so I stepped on it. Looked like a rich guy.

"When are they gonna do something about this traffic?" he wanted to know. "A man can't be on time anymore."

"Dunno," I said.

"A man can't hear himself think anymore," he said. "Makes you want to buy a hearing aid."

"You're right," I said.

"My brother sells hearing aids, you know."

"Yeah?"

It turns out his brother travels all over the country pushing hearing aids off on deaf people. Tells them all about what they're buying too, only they're too deaf to hear him. One thing they wouldn't hear anyway is that there's a little part of the thing made to go bad every six months, so they have to come in twice a year to replace it for twenty-five dollars. What a great racket, the guys says. Some people have all the luck.

"You cabbies got the life all right," he says. "All you do is drive around all day and listen to other people's problems. What's this I hear about a union?"

"Don't know anything about it," I say. "Ain't a union man myself."

"Well, it's a pleasure meeting you then," the guy says. "If there's one thing destroying this country quicker than creeping degeneracy, it's creeping unionism. You know what my secretary said to me today?" Turns out his secretary is one of them feminists. "Said she's quitting if she doesn't get a raise by the end of the week."

"That's tough," I say.

"Yeah, but that's not the half of it. Next week we have the annual board meeting and she's got to be there to take minutes. Now you tell me what I'm gonna do at the annual board meeting without a secretary."

The guy pulls out one of them expensive-looking Meerschaum pipes and lights it. Normally I remind passengers not to smoke but, hell, this one might just take it out of my tip.

"And, wouldn't you know it," he goes on, "the auditor's gonna be there. Says there's a discrepancy in the books, the bastard. I keep telling them it's his lousy auditing, but nobody will believe me, the schmucks."

"That's a shame," I say.

Then he yanks a watch out of his vest pocket and, I swear to God, it looks like it cost five thousand dollars. "I wish you'd step on it, my friend. I'm late for a very important one."

So, I step on it.

"I'm tellin' you, women'll be the downfall of this nation," the guys says, and he starts in on his wife. "My wife's a bitch." Spends all his money. Gabs all the time. Eats like a horse. Lousy in bed.

"Yeah," I say.

"You got it good," he says. "You know what my wife did yesterday?"

Turns out he found a plastic dildo in his wife's drawer, complete with a special pronged ring around the tip and a little bulb attached to a hose for hot water. So he says to his wife, "What the hell is this?" he says. And she tells him that's what she uses to bake cakes with, and then she goes ahead and mixes up the batter and stirs it with the dildo and she puts milk in the hot water bulb and shows him how she squeezes the bulb and it lets her get just the right consistency of batter while she's stirring.

"You believe that?" he says.

"Sounds pretty tall," I say.

Then he leans forward. "There's my stop. You can let me off on the corner."

So, I pull over and put the flag down. "Seven bucks," I tell him.

"You gotta be kidding," he says, and he looks at the meter to check on it. "You raised your fares, didn't you?"

"I guess we did."

"That's unionism for you. What'd I tell you? Well, it'll have to come out of your tip. I know it's not your fault and I'm sorry, but, well, when collectivism takes root it's the individual that suffers." And the guy hands me exactly seven dollars, the cheap skunk.

For the first time I look him in the eye, not believing what I'm hearing. "I'm sorry, but nothing can be done," he blurts, sliding towards the door with his briefcase in tow. "Chalk it up to history."

Well, normally I'm an uncomplaining man. This time, though, everything went purple. I mean, you work hard every night, hacking out a living and keeping your mouth shut, and this dude gets into your cab and tells you to chalk it up to history. Before I even knew what was happening, I'd closed my fist on the can of mace I keep on the dashboard to use against thugs and was pointing it straight at him.

"What's that?" the guy says, looking kinda pale.

"It's to squirt in the faces of customers that don't tip."

So then the guy gulps real hard, pulls out his wallet and hands me fifty cents like he was doling out medicine to a diabetic. That did it. "You're a lousy cheapskate," I say. "Give me your wallet."

Now it's his turn to stare. "What?"

"I said give me your wallet."

"Are you robbing me?"

"Call it what you like," I say.

"But... cabbies don't rob customers!"

"Give me your wallet, you skunk, or you're gettin' a face full of lather that'll make your eyelashes curl for a week."

Then the guy gets real red in the face and drops his wallet in the back seat, but I make him pick it up and hand it to me. And while he's sittin' there mumbling, I go through his wallet and there's all kinds of money in it, but not only that; there are credit cards too. Millions of `em. So I scoop out everything, including his driver's license and social security card. Then I tell him to scram and take off, leaving him standin' on the corner shakin' his fist and choking on my fumes.

I still say the skunk got what he deserved. `Course I can't go back to the garage, so I just start driving down the interstate, charging gas to the guy's credit cards as I go, and the next morning I stop somewhere in Virginia and get the cab painted purple. Then I drive down to Florida where my cousin's a broker and, well, to make a long story short, I've invested in hearing aids. Chalk it up to history.

PRIVATE AFFAIR

I was flying home in the best seat on the plane. It was far enough behind the wing to provide an unrestricted view, and what a view it was; thousands of feet below me and hundreds of miles in each direction stretched an infinite vista of space and land. There I was, calmly observing the silence of the earth rolling gently beneath me like a sigh. The sigh filled me with a longing to capture and preserve the beauty of the moment. So, I opened my bag and pulled out my camera.

I'm a photographer. Wait, that's an understatement; I *live* to take pictures. For as long as I can remember, in fact, it's been central to my well-being. If I couldn't take pictures, well, what would be the point of existing at all?

As I fitted the camera with its wide-angle lens, I could barely take my eyes off the breathtaking view waiting to be photographed. I peered through the viewfinder and snapped five or six shots in quick succession. I aimed the camera at the horizon and squeezed off another five or six, then panned down to get a shot of the ground.

And noticed that it was disturbingly close. Suddenly there was a sickening plunge, so swift and steep that the camera careened upward out of my hands and yanked on its leash. All around me, passengers screamed. Part of me screamed too, but not as loud as my need to take pictures.

I retrieved the camera and started snapping images of those around me. And what dramatic images they were; faces contorted in fear, lips wrapped around terrified screams and bodies sitting in rigid anticipation of imminent destruction.

I kept snapping until, just as suddenly as it had veered into its spiral of death, the plane leveled off and the panic became more muted. All up and down the aisle, baggage and belongings lay strewn. And though their eyes still bore the immutable gleam of terror, their voices had hushed to just below the level of a scream.

"Oh my God," someone muttered, "I thought we would die."

An old woman in front had fainted, and a middle-aged man in the seat behind mine clutched his chest, murmuring that he was in pain. A younger man nearby jumped out of his seat and headed toward the cockpit, intending, he said, to ask for a doctor.

My attention returned to the view out the window as I instinctively moved the camera back to my eye. Now we were even lower than before and, while the passenger in me sensed a tinge of fear, the artist inside felt a bursting of bliss.

Resuming my pan of the world below, I began repeating the earlier sequence of shots from this lower altitude.

That's when the airplane's intercom crackled to life. "Ladies and gentlemen," a voice said as the plane began a series of lazy turns, "this is your captain speaking." The turns gradually narrowed until we were rolling steeply back and forth. "Sorry to get you all involved in this thing. It's really a private affair. I mean, it's... oh hell, never mind. Anyway, there's nothing you can do about it. What's happening is inevitable, so make the best of it; sit back, relax, and enjoy the sensations. Try to remain conscious during your last moments on earth."

Jesus Christ, I thought, the pilot is mad! I couldn't believe what I had just heard. All around me, a stupefied murmur arose as a dull–but not yet panicked–cognition slowly spread through the cabin. The passengers sat in their seats in mummified silence.

Then the youthful man who'd gone to the cockpit suddenly reappeared, making his way clumsily back down the aisle. His face looked pale and his shoulders trembled slightly as he spoke. "The pilot's locked the door," he said. "I think he's crazy. We've got to do something or all of us will die."

Before anyone could respond, the plane went into another nosedive sending him sprawling into his seat. People braced themselves for what would happen. Some closed their eyes, softly crying to themselves. Others wailed. Many prayed.

I turned back to the window. The view sucked the breath right out of my chest. I could still see the last of the sun's rays that I had so joyfully photographed just moments before. Only now I was seeing them from a fresh angle, as if everything had shifted in some uncanny way. The lingering rays decorated the right edge of my viewfinder as, on the left, the sultry earth shimmered. But it was a vertical earth; a marvelous, starlit, infinite, vertical earth. I grabbed my camera and, almost without realizing it, frantically resumed snapping pictures. I may be about to die, I thought, but the first thing the damned mortician will have to do is pry this camera from my cold bloody hands.

But I didn't die. Nobody did, at least not yet. At the last minute, just when it looked like the end, the plane leveled off and the intercom cleared its throat.

"Temporary reprieve," the pilot announced. "I'm sure you're all wondering why this is happening to you. I can't explain it myself; it's just something I have to do. Enjoy this minor break; it's the last gift you'll ever receive."

The only passenger with enough presence of mind to do anything was the young man who'd previously gone forward to knock on the pilot's door. Now he jumped to his feet again and, in a voice loud enough for all to hear, announced, "We've got to act now or none of us will survive! Who'll come with me to break down the door and pull that madman out?"

"But who'll fly the plane?" murmured a passenger who immediately buried his head in his hands and began weeping miserably.

Our self-appointed leader looked furious. Sprinting up the aisle, he grabbed the weeping man by the shoulders and rocked him violently. "I will, you fool, and you'll be my copilot. What we don't know, we'll learn; it's either that or we die. Now stand up and help me break down that door!" He pulled the man to his feet and slapped him hard on the shoulders. "Get yourself together, man," he said.

It was an order, and everyone knew it.

"OK," he went on, more calmly now, "who else is coming up with us? We'll need all the help we can get."

And people started volunteering. "I'll go," said a woman across the aisle from me, standing up. One by one the passengers followed her, joining the growing throng in the aisle until there were more people standing than still in their seats. In fact, I was one of the handful left sitting. I had intended to stand up too, but glanced out the window and became intrigued by the uncanny views staring at me from there. So, I'd picked up my camera, snapped a few preliminary shots and was changing the shutter speed for the next batch when the first of the rebellious passengers passed by. The leader must have noticed me, because suddenly he stopped next to my seat.

"Hey *you*," he said. I looked up absently and saw his finger pointing accusingly at me. "You coming with us to drag that maniac out?"

"Me? Uh... I'm kind of busy right now." I thought if I slowed the shutter speed to $1/30^{th}$ and shot it at F1.4, I might just get the shot.

"What kind of moron are you?" he wanted to know. "Don't you realize your life is in danger?"

"Yes. I mean... uh, no. I understand." Then again, I could shoot it at F2, and try a longer shutter speed. But that might be tricky.

A sharp smack on the side of my head disrupted all concentration. I looked up and saw that the man rendering it was the same one who, moments before, had been whimpering that no one knew how to fly. He wanted to hit me again, but the leader restrained him. "Nah, don't," he said. "We'll take care of him later."

Then they left, rushing toward the cockpit. I decided on 1/30th at F1.4 and got ready to shoot the horizon. But not before sneaking a quick shot at the receding band of heroes.

I guess that's where the story ends. I'm still sitting here taking pictures and I believe they are excellent. I'm happy with my life as a photographer. Sometimes, though, during particularly steep nosedives, I fear that I might not survive. In those moments, I think of the swarm of rebellious passengers that set off toward the cockpit and wonder if they'll succeed. I guess I want them to. Maybe they'll make better pilots than the idiot up there now. I worry, though, about what that would do to the quality of my pictures.

THE CREVICE

"Look between the rocks," the old woman said, leaning against an overhanging ledge and sipping lemonade from a straw. "Look hard."

But the young girl, peering intently into the crevice, saw only the dark-lit interior of a miniature gray cave. "I see nothing," she said.

The old woman took two quick sucks, making a gurgling sound as she did, and casually brushed a long wisp of gray hair from out of her eye. "Let me have a look," she said. She carefully lay the paper cup aside and plopped herself onto her knees to peer into the tiny crack between the rocks.

It was a beautiful fall day and, glancing at the sky, the girl saw a cloud in the shape of spectacles. "See anything, Grandma?" she asked.

Lost in concentration, the old woman kept her silence. "Hold on a minute while I get my bearings," she said finally, wiggling her bottom just a little. "My eyes aren't as good as they used to be. Wait a minute. No... No... Nope, can't say I see anything at all." She lifted her head and looked at the girl. "Just because we can't see him," the old woman said, "doesn't mean he's not there."

"How many times have *you* seen him?" the girl wanted to know.

The old woman paused thoughtfully before answering. "Enough to know he's real," she said. She sat down against the rock, picked up her lemonade and took a few furious sips. Then she rested her head against the rock wall, letting her eyes wander lazily over the landscape. "See that river?" she said after a while. "When I was just a girl, younger than you, I used to go swimming in that river." She swallowed, eying her audience curiously.

"How many times have you seen him, Grandma?" the girl persisted with a little more urgency.

A smile began at the edges of the old woman's face and slowly spread upward. To the girl it seemed to cover a secret, some private amusement that she hoped the old woman would share.

"The first time I saw him was right *here*," the grandma said. "My daddy brought me. We took a canoe up the river and came ashore right over there." She made a wide sweep with her arm, indicating a spot on the riverbank. "Then we came right up through those rushes to this rock, and that's where I first saw him. I've seen him lots of times since then."

A fly landed on the old woman's cheek, and she swatted it away. "It's not something everyone sees. Lots of people would say you're crazy if you ever told them."

"You're not crazy!" the young girl assured her grandma.

The old woman chuckled. "Your mom might disagree. If she knew we were here, she'd yell at me for sure."

The girl had heard the story often. How her grandmother had come to the bank of the river and claimed to see God. How she had talked about it so much that her family eventually grew weary until finally, years later, her own daughter—by then almost grown—had cursed the heavens, and declared herself an atheist.

"I don't think you're crazy," the girl repeated.

Suddenly the old woman grew serious. "You've got to promise me," she said. "This here's our secret place. Promise that you'll never tell."

"I promise," the girl said solemnly.

"Not even your mom," the old woman said. "*Especially* not your mom."

"Cross my heart," the girl said.

The old woman smiled. "It's a deal then," she said, putting the paper cup down and struggling to her feet.

"Let's have another look. This time you have to *concentrate*."

The girl fell to her knees and stared rigidly into the black crevice, but saw nothing. She squinted and blinked twice. Still nothing. "Pick a spot," the old woman said, kneeling beside her. The girl picked a point directly on the back wall of the little cave and focused all her attention on it. It began moving, and she blinked hard to keep it in place but failed.

"It's swimming," the girl said.

"Follow it," the old woman instructed.

The spot seemed to swim in giant, lazy circles. The girl followed it with her eyes until it had completed a loop and stopped directly at the bottom of the cave, then disappeared.

"It disappeared," she reported.

"No, it hasn't." the old woman insisted.

The girl stared at the place where the spot had been, peering into the blackness as if her life depended on it. Ten seconds passed. Then suddenly she saw it, as if out of nowhere; a barely discernable footprint, dimly lit but otherwise perfect in every detail. It was unmistakable.

"A f*ootprint*!" the girl whispered, afraid to blink an eye

The old woman beamed. "That's right," she said, "It's *his* footprint. Do you see anything else?"

The girl stared into the crevice with all her might, but could see nothing. "Where is he?" she whispered. "Where can I find him?"

The old woman chuckled and patted the young girl's shoulder. "*Anywhere*," she said. "E*verywhere*. Sometimes it takes a long time. You've seen his footprint already; One day, if you're good, you might see the rest of him."

She took hold of the girl's hand and gently drew her away from the crevice in the rock. "We'll come back tomorrow," the old woman said. "Maybe by then he'll be here himself."

THE NARROW CYLINDER

The cylinder you're tucked into is eight miles deep and two feet wide, but you like it down here. Despite the heaviness, it's nice lying under all this silence.

One day a face appears at the mouth of your confinement: a tiny face peering down at you from eight miles high. You wish it would go away, but it won't. It smiles and calls, "Hey, *you*," as the echo reverberates back and forth against the miles of aluminum separating you from the face. "Hey, *you-u-u*," the voice calls, "why not come out of there?"

You want to answer, but don't have the strength. You want to tell the face to go away and mind its own business, but you can't. "Hey down there," it repeats, "want to escape? I can help."

Enough already, you think.

"Trust me," the voice calls, "I will free you. I am *coming-g-g.*"

Your cells murmur their opposition, but it's barely audible, even to you. Let them try, you think. You feel the weight of all that space pressing every inch of you downward and back. How nice this weight feels, you think, how like a blanket. Let them try, you yawn; how nice this weight.

Later you awake with a buzzing in your ears, or is it? It goes on and on, incessant, like a... *something*. At first, it's faint, but gradually the volume increases. You can't think, and suddenly you know what that sound is; incessant, like a... *drill*.

The final drilling has begun.

It sounds like a mantra. Slyly, it seeps into your consciousness, systematically displacing the other occupants of your mind one by one. Efficiently, steadily, it permeates your head until there is no room for anything else and the refugees of your mind slip into the gloomy spaces between you and that confounded wall. The buzzing is inside you now and, yet, it persists, secretly creeping along the gangways of your brain seeking sanctuary, grasping for the hollow quiet place hidden deep within your center. Everything is buzzing, humming, churning. You know that the drill is close, and your fingers shake. Somewhere inside you, a tiny voice spits static; "Convergence imminent, critical juncture!"

Please stop, you think, please let me be.

But the voice gets louder, repeating its warning in a more urgent tone. "Convergence imminent! Assume readiness..."

"Please," you want to say, but the voice gets there first. "*Convergence!*"

Quick as a flash, the white-hot tip of the drill shaft penetrates the wall, shattering the peace of your cocoon in a beam of seething light. Lord God how it stabs!

In the operating room, a surgeon withdraws his sharp buzzing instrument and shakes his head. His shoulders slump as an assistant removes his glasses, wipes them clean and replaces them on his face. Then he glances at a clock on the wall. "Time of death," he says, "3:26. May your journey be swift."

ACKNOWLEDGMENTS

First, I wish to thank my daughter and editor, Adina Haldane Morgan, for the hours she spent reading and reacting to these stories. Her input was invaluable, and many of her suggestions were incorporated into the final draft. I also wish to thank my oldest and best friend, Ron Featheringill, whose appreciation inspired confidence. And, finally, my publisher, Reagan Rothe, who asked if I had anything lying around that might be publishable and, lo, I did! Beyond that, I want to express my appreciation to all the people–past and present–whose character, thoughts, words, and actions inspired these stories. You know who you are and if you don't, well, thank you anyway.

ABOUT THE AUTHOR

David Haldane, a former *Los Angeles Times* staff writer, authored the award-winning memoir *Nazis & Nudists*. In addition to his journalism, essays and short fiction, Haldane has written and produced radio features for which he was awarded a Golden Mike by the Radio & Television News Association of Southern California. He currently divides his time between homes in Joshua Tree, California, and Northern Mindanao, Philippines where he writes a weekly newspaper column called "Expat Eye."

NOTE FROM THE AUTHOR

Word-of-mouth is crucial for any author to succeed. If you enjoyed *Jenny on the Street*, please leave a review online—anywhere you are able. Even if it's just a sentence or two. It would make all the difference and would be very much appreciated.

Thanks!

David Haldane

Thank you so much for reading one of David Haldane's titles.
If you enjoyed our book, please check out our recommendation
for your next great read!

Nazis & Nudists by David Haldane

"Haldane's storytelling is rapid, fact-packed, devoid of filler
(and) heavy on action."
-Long Beach Press Telegram

"The story is unflinching, wildly improbable
and pretty scary in spots."
-Ken Borgers, *Ksds 88.3 San Diego*

View other Black Rose Writing titles at
www.blackrosewriting.com/books and use promo code
PRINT to receive a **20% discount** when purchasing.